BENDS AND TURNS

Leena Chandorkar

FROG BOOKS

ISBN 978-93-52017-30-0

First published in India 2016 by Frog Books
An imprint of Leadstart Publishing Pvt Ltd
1 Level, Trade Centre
Bandra Kurla Complex
Bandra (East) Mumbai 400 051 India
Telephone: +91-22-40700804
Fax: +91-22-40700800
Email: info@leadstartcorp.com
www.leadstartcorp.com / www.frogbooks.net

Sales Office:
Unit No.25/26, Building No.A/1,
Near Wadala RTO,
Wadala (East), Mumbai – 400037 India
Phone: +91 22 24046887

US Office:
Axis Corp, 7845 E Oakbrook Circle
Madison, WI 53717 USA

Editor: Tina Khatri
Cover: Randhir Khare
Layouts: Chandravadan R. Shiroorkar

Typeset in Palatino Linotype
Printed at Repro

For my parents,
Brigadier Madhukar Prachand (Retd) and Ratnaprabha Prachand

Acknowledgements

Writing is a lonely and solitary job, yet so many people have helped in the completion of this book, that I cannot claim it to be mine alone.

My dear parents, who gifted me a wonderful childhood, deserve my first thanks.

Randhir Khare, poet at large and mentor for many, who read the first draft and brutally told me to rewrite it all over again. And what a wise piece of advice it was! He read through the second draft, gave valuable suggestions and told me to go ahead with publication. I can't thank him enough for his generosity.

Dr Vaishali Naik, good friend and gentle critic, who read the MS and gave productive feedback ... Thanks dear!

Dr Rajmohan from Sahitya Akademi, who made me revise the synopsis again and again and regaled me with horror stories about publishers. Thank you for everything.

The team at Leadstart: Uzair Thakur and Tina Khatri, who have lent prompt support and professional help. Thank you Malini Nair for liking the book and taking it on.

I thank my husband Sarang for always being a rock of support, for believing in me and never underestimating me. Mihika, my dear daughter, you brighten up my life and make it all worthwhile.

Finally, a big thank you to all the interesting people who crisscrossed my path and left a mark. Please people, do not try to identify yourself in the book! The characters are entirely fictitious!

asato ma sadgamaya
tamaso ma jyotirgamaya
mrtyorma amrtam gamaya

Lead me from untruth to truth.
Lead me from darkness to light.
Lead me from death to immortality.

(Brhadaranyaka Upanishad — I.iii.28)

PART-I

1

She ended the call, but could not stop trembling. She felt again like a spanked child. Fighting the feelings of rebellion, anger, pain, she pouted and brushed her tears away. It was time for her to move out from the high magnetic field surrounding her mother. *This* was her life now…This beautiful bungalow, the furniture, and the lovely garden was her life. She was the proud mistress of it all.

She stepped into her dew-soaked garden. Dara was following her, wagging his tail, sniffing the flowerbeds, and bounding around.

"Ganpat!" she called out, "Take Dara out now. He's restless today!"

Ganpat came out from the garage, where he was cleaning the BMW. "He doesn't look restless to me!" he said, but put a leash on Dara and took him out nevertheless. His wife Champabai came out of the outhouse with her six-year old son Chhotu.

"Not gone to school yet?" Sona asked the little boy.

"He's not feeling well today vahini saheb. So I've kept him home," Champabai replied, and hurried inside the big house.

Sona breathed in the fresh, flower-scented air deeply. This was her domain, and she was the queen of all she surveyed. Everything was going well in her world and she was happy. Of course, she was happy.

Rajeev had already left for the factory. Seven-thirty. Always seven-thirty. You could set the clock with his comings and goings. He stepped into the office at eight. Always eight. His subordinates had to be in office fifteen minutes before he arrived. He couldn't abide unpunctuality. He was the boss and he laid down the rules. Inviolable and cast in stone. Discipline was a big deal with him. So very like my Mother actually, Sona thought. But he chose me as his wife. Me, who is so unlike my Mother. She smiled as she clipped a twining creeper and put it in her cane basket. The heart has its reasons, she thought as she plucked the mogras one by one. Why did I choose someone who shared my Mother's traits to be my husband? She clipped the yellow rose carefully, keeping the thorns away. Her cane basket looked joyous and colourful with leaves, creepers, and flowers. "Thank you garden," she said to herself and walked inside the house, stepping in through the wide French windows into the dining room. She set the glass bowls and vases before her and started arranging the greenery. She gave the task her full concentration, thinking of nothing else except arranging the flowers beautifully. After the flower arrangement was completed, she placed the bowls and vases in the room. The spacious hall smiled in gratitude and she smiled back. She carefully gathered up the cuttings to throw into the compost pit outside.

An hour spent contentedly in her garden. An hour spent bringing her home alive. An hour spent adding beauty to this space. An hour wasted, as Mother would say. And to be frank, who cared whether she brought beauty into this home or not? There were hardly any visitors. Rajeev left early and returned late. He hardly ever noticed. If she never did any flower arrangement in her life again, nobody would notice. Waste of time, as Mother would say.

Why did the thought of Mother agitate her so? Was it because secretly she found a grain of truth in it? "But I'm nothing like my mother," Sona said to herself. "There is no talent that is going to waste because of my being here. What do I have to offer the world anyway?" She looked out from her first floor bedroom. Suddenly, the sky had become overcast. As she gazed out, she saw water drops falling down and it started drizzling. She shut the window and gazed at the rain. She really ought to go for her shower. She chose a bright salwar-kameez to combat the darkening mood gathering within her and went into the bathroom.

Showered and dressed, it was still only ten in the morning. The day yawned before her. She could hear Champabai sweeping the ground floor. She decided to clear the cupboards in her room. She took out the outfits from the shelves and started arranging them in three piles. The first pile was of clothes to be given away, the second pile was to be thrown away and the last pile had clothes that would be retained. Recently, online shopping had her hooked, and in a month's time, she had accumulated many clothes that she no longer liked or needed. Champabai walked in just as she was done with the top shelf. "Vahini saheb, not again!" Champabai said "You cleaned the cupboard just two months ago!"

"It's a dusty town!" Sona said, "Cockroaches breed fast in this weather."

"Not even cockroaches can breed so fast!" Champabai mumbled.

"What did you say?"

"Nothing...!" Champabai said, and swooped down to sweep under the bed.

A year ago, when Sona had entered this house as a new bride, Ganpat, Champabai and Chhotu were already living in the outhouse, and taking care of Rajeev saheb and his house and garden. Sona was the newcomer and it took her some time to lay down new rules and run the house according to her rhythm. But for Ganpat and Champabai she would always be the new bride. The woman their Rajeev saheb brought home. He kept her like a queen, Ganpat and Champabai told each other. He had bought a BMW for her though she had nowhere to go. Yet she never seemed happy. And especially after last month's incident, things were not all well between the two. "What else does she want from her husband?" they asked each other, "Saheb earns well, does not beat her, showers gifts on her...what else does she want?"

Meanwhile, Sona had finished with the cupboard and felt like having a cup of coffee. It was still only eleven-thirty. She went down to the kitchen, poured the water in the coffee machine and started looking for the filter paper. Oh, she had used the last one yesterday, but a new packet was kept somewhere. She opened drawers to find the packet of filter paper. As she opened the cupboard next to the fridge, she spotted the burnt-out stub of the mermaid candle. Her heart heaved as she looked at it. She picked up the stub and held it to her bosom and large tears dropped unbidden from her eyes on to the melted contours of the wax mermaid.

Champabai bustled in just then and saw her in tears. "Vahini!" Champabai dropped the broom and came to her, "Sit down Vahini! You should have told me na, if you wanted coffee! Sit here now! I'll make a hot cup for you!"

Sona allowed Champabai to lead her to the dining room and sat down obediently. The happenings of that fateful day in the last month swam before her eyes.

2

It was their first wedding anniversary. Sona was excited and woke up early. She looked at the sleeping figure next to her. He lay on his back. She reached out and stroked his face. He frowned and turned, leaving her with an expanse of back. He hated to be touched in sleep. There was always a designated space around him that was his space. Inviolable! Unbreachable! He reached out to her only when he wanted, never otherwise. She withdrew her hand, as though stung. Her touch was unwelcome. She felt the rejection. She would not touch him again, she said to herself, unless he wanted it. With that resolution made, she got up, and went into the bathroom to brush her teeth. She was soon out and went down to prepare tea. When she re-entered the room some time later with a tray of tea and biscuits, Rajeev was still asleep. She put down the tray on the side table and sat down near him. Smiling dreamily, she stroked a thick lock of hair away from his forehead and whispered in his ear, "Wake up! Tea is ready!"

He opened his eyes in an unfocused gaze. "What's the time?" he mumbled. His gaze travelled to the bedside clock and he jumped out of bed as though stung. "Seven o'clock!" he shouted, "I'm late! There is no time for my run now! Why didn't you wake me earlier?" He had already grabbed his towel and was moving towards the bathroom, when Sona held his hand and stopped his headlong progress.

"Don't you remember what day it is?" she pouted, "Can't you go a bit late one day?"

"What day?"

"It is our first wedding anniversary of course!"

"Oh yeah!" he said, "Of course!" He came over and brushed his lips against her cheek. "And now I really must go Sona! I'll be home early today, I promise." With that, he was already in the bathroom and she was staring at the shut door.

Sighing, she picked up her cup and took a sip. They did not want to go out and so she had decided to do all the cooking for tonight's dinner herself. So, she would be busy with Champabai in the kitchen in the morning, cooking the dishes for the evening. She had given the evening off to Ganpat and Champabai, who in any case wanted to visit an ailing relative in the nearby village.

She picked up the framed photograph on the side table. It was clicked two years ago and already it seemed a long time back. Rajeev was laughing in it. His dark hair had flopped over his forehead. He was wearing a black turtleneck sweater and the bright sun etched his sharp features into classic angles. He was looking into the distance. She was next to him, looking not at the camera but at him. They were laughing. Both of them were looking young, lovely and very much in love. It was a beautiful candid shot taken by Monica's brother, Shaan.

Rajeev was officially Monica's boyfriend at that time. But Shaan guessed the secret that Sona had thought she had hidden well and brought it out in this photograph. Rajeev and Monica had broken up soon after this picnic and Sona had drawn closer to Rajeev. He was five years older than she was. He was an engineer, who was working with a multinational company. He came from a humble background, but that was not the reason why Mother objected to him.

Actually, there was nothing to object about him. He was young, handsome, an IIT graduate, holding a wonderful job at a big multinational. The problem was that he had made the terrible mistake of falling in love with Sona, daughter of Kamla Pradhan, MP, which meant that he would be taking her away from her goals, and the career path that her mother had chalked out for her. Any man wanting to take Sona away would have had to face the ire of Kamla Pradhan, MP.

Sona sighed again and kept the photo back on the table. "Think again," Mother had told her, "Think long term. What is there for you in that backward Shivagaon where your dear Rajeev has his factory? Love will sustain you for a year at the most, and then…and then what will you do? Rajeev will get busier and you will have nothing but empty hours to hold on to. Look at yourself Sona! You are at the threshold of an exciting career. You have the offer of working as an editor of a new youth magazine. You have the opportunity to build it up from scratch. Why throw it all away for an unpredictable future?"

Sona looked at her Mother with round eyes. "You must be the only mother I know who doesn't want her grown-up daughter to get married. Mothers of all my friends are urging them every day to get hitched. And here you are, beating away a perfectly eligible young man who wants to marry your daughter. Don't you want grandchildren Mother?"

Her mother had blown a fuse then. She was not used to being answered back like this. "It is not about what I want. It is about what is good for you. I do not see things short-term. I've lived longer in this world and have stopped seeing it with rose-tinted glasses."

"Well, for once let me look at the world through my own glasses, rose-tinted or otherwise." Sona said, feeling amazed herself at her own audacity and stormed out in a rage.

Rajeev was a hard-won prize. A prize won after a prolonged tug-of-war with her mother. The more Mother protested against the marriage, the more persistent Sona became. Eventually, Rajeev and marriage with him became the simplest way out of the strong control of her mother. Therefore, Sona hurried him into a commitment for which he was perhaps not yet ready. But after making the commitment he held her hand, so tightly in fact, that it was as if Mother had never left her hand at all!

Sona came back to the present with a jerk, and went downstairs calling out urgently to Champabai.

As she supervised the dusting and cleaning of the house, she imagined how the evening would pan out. She had already decided on the sari. Rajeev liked her in saris and though secretly she thought that she was too thin for saris, she had collected a horde of them in the last year in deference to Rajeev's choice.

She went into the kitchen to prepare the special dal that reminded Rajeev of his mother's cooking. She took out the vegetables from the fridge for the pulao and while Champabai busily chopped them, Sona opened the tin of gulab jamuns to pour them into a glass bowl. For an hour and a half, the two women worked with cheerful busyness. Sona enjoyed cooking occasionally like this, though she was glad to have Champabai to take care of the daily cooking. Breakfast and lunch were solitary affairs on weekdays and consequently light. They did not eat out much, partly because there were not many fancy restaurants in this area. Shivagaon was a newly developed industrial belt. Factory owners like Rajeev had set up Industrial units here and the Rotary club comprised of these factory owners and small-scale industrialists. Their wives formed a motley group, which tried listlessly to organise get-togethers and dos during festivals. Sona tried hard to gel with the crowd, but apart from Pushpa, she had been unable to make a friend in this place.

Therefore, Sona spent the days by keeping the house beautiful, reading the thick books that she had always longed to read but could never find the leisure to, watching TV and yes, waiting…

She waited endlessly for Rajeev's phone call, for the sound of his car turning inside the gate, and the sound of his quick footsteps as he entered the porch, and for his voice as he called out, "Sona! I'm home!"

Finally all the major dishes for the evening were prepared. Sona put them into microwave-safe bowls and stowed them into the fridge. She would prepare the rotis just before they sat down for dinner. Everything else was ready, she would heat and serve the dishes in the evening.

Meanwhile she could do with a glass of milk and cookies. She took this sparse breakfast into the porch outside and had it slowly, watching Dara sniffing around the flowerbeds and Ganpat watering the plants.

"Pushpa was talking of developing a cactus garden," Sona thought absently, "Not a bad idea. I can have a rock garden in the corner too. Maybe plant succulents. Why not call a horticulturist to landscape the garden! But I can do that too…only I'll need some advice as to the care and upkeep of the seasonal flowers. Maybe I can join a course on landscaping at the Agriculture College here. I should ask Rajeev about it. Why has Rajeev not called today? He generally calls around this time, when they have a coffee break. He seemed preoccupied in the morning too. Hope all is well with that factory of his. He has a hefty loan to repay. I do not much trust his accounts chief. He does not seem competent enough. But Rajeev doesn't speak much about him. Come to think of it… Rajeev doesn't talk much about that factory of his with me.

Whom does he share his anxiety with then? Preeti, his secretary is close to him, professionally of course. He said himself that he can trust Preeti with the most sensitive of documents and rest in peace that they were safe with her. He is lucky to have a trustworthy secretary. A secretary can make or break the career of any boss. Hmm…she must be quite young. Twenty-six? Twenty-five? Seems like a nice girl. Not Rajeev's type of course. But who can tell with men?"

Suddenly, Sona got up and called out sharply to Ganpat.

"Ganpat! Watch out! Dara is trampling the plants in the flowerbeds! You have spoiled him too much, you know that! He should know his place!"

She stamped into the house, her mood prickly for some strange reason. Mother had called in the morning itself to wish her on her anniversary. She had an important meeting today with the French Minister for Civil Aviation and probably that was the reason why she sounded excited and preoccupied. She talked of this and that and described the wonderful function she had attended last evening at the Rashtrapati Bhavan ---the President's 'At Home' for all the winners of the awards given away on the occasion of Republic Day. Sona yawned, already bored. "Wonder why Mother is going so ga-ga over this At Home!" she thought, "Not that this is the first function she is attending at the Rashtrapati Bhavan!" Nevertheless, she made appropriately polite noises and the conversation ended soon enough as such conversations generally did between them.

After she had showered and dressed, she had a light lunch and sat down to check her e-mail. She kept in touch with some of her ex-colleagues from the *News* days. There was a mail from Sarita. Sarita was the only one who kept her updated about *News*. A change of regime had taken place soon after Sona left *News*. Mr. Tiwari replaced the old editor, Papa Lobo. He was as different from Papa Lobo as jeans could be from a dhoti! Sarita had written that there was a vacancy in *News* at the junior editorial level. Sona could try her luck! "Silly girl," Sona thought, "Doesn't she know that my world is here at Shivagaon now? I am a married woman now, with responsibilities and duties!" But still, Sona read the advertisement carefully.

"What's the harm in applying?" Sarita had written, "You can always refuse, if the terms are not suitable. But you should not be left with regret, with the feeling of 'what if!'"

"Clever Sarita! Must be feeling lonely without me," Sona thought affectionately.

As she lay down for a short nap, she picked up the book on the Peshwas that she had bought on her last visit to Mumbai.

"It was an extremely well-written book. Such beautiful language! And the painstaking research! What must have driven this British scholar to devote so many years of his life to the research of Maratha history," she thought, "A junoon! Something more than just academic curiosity. Wish I had a junoon like this! Wish I could be possessed by a madness to throw myself completely into a project!"

"Unfortunately I'm too balanced to go unhinged like this!" she sighed. This kind of madness requires one to forego the safety of the shore and launch into the turbulent seas. She remembered her swimming coach yelling to her to let go of the safety rail on the side of the swimming pool.

"You'll never learn to swim if you don't let go of the safety rail!" he had shouted. To just be possessed by a dream, to throw oneself into it headlong! How does it feel?

Unbidden, Rajeev's face came to her mind. *Geeta Engineering Works*--- the junoon that drove Rajeev Jayakar!

Her eyes closed after a while and she slept. When she awoke, it was almost four. She got up and made herself tea. Then she allowed herself to flow with the rhythm of the evening. A quiet time of the day, in which she did her favourite things. She did puja as the sun sank, the tinkle of the bell blending seamlessly with the waning day. She looked at the beloved deities in her puja ghar and thanked god again for all that she had been blessed with. Then leaving the room fragrant with the scent of sandalwood incense sticks and mogra flower garlands that Champabai had strung in the morning, she came out into the porch. One by one, she put on the garden lights, the light in the porch and the lights in the driveway. The garden came alive, looked festive, the little solar lights strung over the champa bush blinked cheerfully. Rajeev's passion! Solar lights! He was forever hunting for different kinds on his trips abroad. She came in and put on the lights inside the house. There was a sequence to how she put on the lights. She liked to follow that sequence. Ganpat and family were out this evening and no sound came from the outhouse. Dara was sitting regally in the porch, looking relaxed and content. She would take a leisurely shower now. Dress carefully.

As she pleated her delicate mauve chiffon sari, she looked at herself in the reflection…she looked changed today, her darkness giving her a sensuality she had not noticed or appreciated before. She glowed, as though a bulb was lit inside her. Her bare arms in the sleeveless blouse glistened with youth and health. She tucked in the pleats and adjusted the pallu. She applied her signature scent, mild but lingering. As she sprayed the scent liberally, she looked at her reflection in the long mirror. For the first time she thought that she looked desirable. A woman! A woman ready for love!

She came down to the hall and looked speculatively at the dining table. She had laid the beautiful white lace tablecloth that her Aunt got her from the US and that she had reserved for special occasions. What can be more special than your first wedding anniversary? She had also brought out her best dinner set. The crystal glasses glistened and tea-lights were waiting to be lighted up in their small glass holders. She thought for a moment and opened a small cupboard next to the fridge. There lay the pink wax mermaid, wrapped in cellophane.

It was another gift from the same aunt. She took out the candle from the paper and looked again at the sweet face of the mermaid, her wax hair etched lovingly by some far-away artist, the scales in her fishy tail painstakingly drawn. "You are too beautiful to be burnt!" she said to the lovely mermaid, "But you are created so that someone will burn you...a memorable burning you'll have mermaid...you'll light up my special day!" With a sigh and a smile, she carried the candle to the dining table. Placing the mermaid at the centre of the table, she ran a finger over the naked contours of her waxy body and said to her, "I'll light you when we sit down to dinner! You were made for this day!"

It was already seven, but she had half-expected Rajeev would not keep his promise today also, so she put on some music on the system. As the soulful strains of the Strauss waltz filled the room, she allowed the music to seep into her being. She lay back on the couch, careful not to crumple her sari and closed her eyes, imagining beautiful snow-capped peaks reaching out to a blue sky dappled with little woolly clouds. The air was so pure, so fresh. She got up and poured herself half a glass of red wine. She was an eagle now, soaring over the Swiss mountains, allowing the wind under her wings to lift her up, up until she could almost look beyond the mountains to the horizon. She poured herself some more wine. It was almost ten... Rajeev had not replied to her two calls… instead of feeling worried, she was angry…a strange reluctance stopped her from calling him again…she took up the

lighter and lighted the wax mermaid. The violins in the background pulled at her heartstrings. She watched thick drops of wax roll down the naked contours of the mermaid. A tear rolled down Sona's cheek too…but she fiercely brushed it away…"Burn!" She said to the mermaid, as her pretty face started to collapse, "Burn! Because that is what you are meant for! To give light through your destruction! In your destruction is your salvation!" And a great sob rose within her, as she went about the house, putting off all the lights one by one. Dara stood in the porch outside, looking in at her through the mesh door and whimpering, sensing her mood. She let him in and he immediately came and sat by her.

"Oh Dara! Dara!" she said, as she sank down next to him, "How could I be stupid enough to have given over the reins of my life to someone who does not love me? All this tasty dinner, this white tablecloth, these beautiful flowers in crystal vases, this chiffon sari… who am I fooling? I am just playing house Dara, and no one needs me here! Not even you…not even you!"

She put her arms around the big dog and buried her face in his strong, furry back. This is how Rajeev found her…fast asleep and dead drunk…when he entered the house two hours later, dishevelled and dirty.

3

The train started with a jerk and a pang of anxiety stabbed her heart. It had been a precipitous decision to leave Shivagaon like this. She had sounded off Rajeev last week when she received the appointment letter from *News*.

"So? Are you joining?" he had asked. She had just shrugged her shoulders. "I am not sure," was all she had said. He never discussed the topic further and she never brought it up again. Yesterday, Sarita called her up and talked to her for half an hour. She shot down all of Sona's feeble excuses. The result was that here was Sona, sitting in a train, after having sent a hurried message to Rajeev who was in Bangalore.

Sona had a window seat. She looked out at the small railway platform, at the ticket counter as it slowly moved away from her area of vision, at the tiny book cart, the water pump, and then the yellow board with 'Shivagaon' written in black in three languages. It was just a three-hour train ride from Shivagaon to Mumbai but it took her from Bharat to India. The pace in Shivagaon was the same as it probably had been fifty or even a hundred years ago. People could survive on very little money. Time slowed down in Shivagaon. But every mile covered towards Mumbai hurtled her towards the Twenty First century to the India with complete network coverage, 4G connectivity, fast food eateries and cabs on order. It took Sona a while to orient herself towards the pace of the two places.

Sona looked out of her train window. The train was leaving behind miles of barren land. It stopped for a very short time at a little station. Sona did not see any passengers getting in, but saw the stationmaster hurrying towards the train engine. It was a very small station, with hardly any activity. As the train slowly picked up speed and left the platform behind, Sona saw the house of the stationmaster. The house was small, like most government allotted houses. A charpoy was placed outside the house, on which sat a youngish woman with a baby in her lap. A little girl in long pigtails and wearing a yellow frock was flitting in and out. The train moved on but the little tableau stuck in Sona's mind. The young woman, whose name was Savitri, was lonely in this little village. She had no neighbours or friends for socialising. She spent her day cooking, cleaning and looking after Saguna and Sonya. She longed for her village by the river. The river was her friend. She sat by the river whenever she felt lonely.

Before she got married, it was by the river that she met her friends. By the river they washed clothes, gossiped and teased each other. It was by the river that she dreamt of a dashing young man who would carry her away in his strong arms, marry her and give her all the happiness of the world... Give her all the riches, the pearls, the gold, the diamonds and the silks. At the right time, a young man did come to her house with his parents and asked for her hand and her father gave her away to the most eligible bachelor in their community. He had a railway job, a permanent government job. He would take care of her. Keep her safe. Make her happy. And so, here she was! Savitri from Ambegaon village, who married the stationmaster of Nasrapur. She was taking care of Saguna and Sonya. She was the queen and mistress of a little government railway house.

Sona realised that the man sitting opposite her was eyeing her curiously and she hurriedly wiped away the tears that were rolling down her cheeks. She must learn to control her emotions, which were always simmering nowadays, threatening to boil over and carry her away in a flood of tears.

She had called up Nafisa last night and told her about her plans. She had told her not to bother coming to the station to pick her up. It was too much to expect people to pick up and drop off friends and relatives in Mumbai.

She would find her way to Nafisa's place on her own. She had been there once or twice. In any case, she was planning to take a taxi to her house. Mumbai was her place, yet these out-of-the-way places still intimidated her. For the last so many years, she had never used public transport. Mother was the Chief Minister of Maharashtra then. Therefore, a chauffeur took Sona around the city, along with security!

"But now starts my independent phase!" Sona thought, and wondered why the thought troubled her. She was so unlike her mother. She wished that she had inherited her mother's decisive nature and firm resolution. "Life is so easy for such authoritative people", Sona thought. She knew that she was nothing like her mother. She was like her poor father, dark and small like him. She was quiet and unassertive, like him. "Why did such two very different people ever marry each other?" she thought. Mother was like Indira Gandhi, imperious and regal. And Baba? Baba had always paled beside her. He disappeared in the light of her radiance. "What must have possessed him to marry her?" she thought. Mother always regarded him as a loser. And it was true that nothing in his life worked. All that he touched turned to ashes, including his various jobs, his business, his farming, and his marriage. Even his heart gave way. Sona believed firmly that he died of a broken heart. She was his only child. She should have been there for him. But carried away with the buoyancy of her own youthful life, she had forgotten all about the father, who was a nominal presence in her life anyway. She had visited him rarely in his village in Ratnagiri district and called him sporadically on less busy weekends. She should have been by his side during his illness, Sona thought distractedly. But one can never imagine one's parents dead. It is only after we lose them that we realise the hole in our lives. They are so much a part of our being that one takes them for granted. "My sole and primary caregiver was my mother," Sona thought, "And all my life I've tried to run away from her."

"What will be Mother's reaction to this decision of mine?" Sona thought, but suppressed the feeling of apprehension that rose within her. "It is *my* decision," she thought fiercely, "to be faced by myself alone."

As the train neared Mumbai, Sona's heart started thumping rapidly. A crowd surged towards the exit at VT station. Sona felt weighed down by the suitcase that she trundled along and the haversack on her back. Her handbag kept slipping off her shoulder and the station seemed hot and sticky after the AC confines of the train compartment. Wiping away the beads of sweat from her forehead with her arm, she took a deep breath and started marching along with the crowd. In a sea of people, Sona felt suddenly alone. Just then, she heard a familiar voice call out her name. A smile leapt to her lips and relief swept over her entire being as she saw the tall and slim figure of Nafisa striding towards her. "Nafisa!" she breathed, "You came for me!"

Nafisa took the suitcase from her hands and took her arm in a firm grip. She guided Sona towards the exit, making her way expertly through the turgid crowd. Out in the open, Sona took gulps of air and looked at Nafisa with shining eyes. Nafisa gave her a warm hug and said, "Welcome back Sona!"

The two friends then made their way towards the parking lot. Nafisa belted herself to the seat and reversed her red SUV in a smooth arc. Sona watched with admiration as Nafisa negotiated her way out of the cramped parking with a little cajoling and a little bullying. As she hit the main road, she picked up speed and Sona leaned back in her seat, content once again to hand over controls to somebody else.

Nafisa drove confidently. "Just like Mother!" Sona thought. Mother loved to drive. Though she went around nowadays in her official vehicle, she took out her beloved sleek black Honda City as often as she could. She loved going on long drives. Her best and most intimate conversations with Mother had been during drives---with Mother driving and Sona in the passenger seat. Perhaps because that was when Mother was most relaxed.

Sona turned towards Nafisa. "You drive well Nafisa!" she said affectionately. And just as she completed her sentence, Nafisa gave a whoop and stepped onto the accelerator. Sona saw that her eyes were set on the traffic lights, which had just turned amber. "Don't Nafisa! Do not! We will not be able to make it. There's a cop standing there!" But Nafisa just kept going. She cleared the junction just as the lights turned red and the traffic from the other side surged forward. "Nafisa!" Sona scolded,

"Just when I had finished complimenting you on your driving skills, you do this mad stunt and take my breath away! Is nothing in life predictable?!"

"Nothing is predictable!" Nafisa sang, "Nothing! Nothing!"

"You seem to be in high spirits! What's the secret?"

"Time to talk later", Nafisa said, "Now my job is to drive and reach you home safely…"

"Yes, stress the safely," Sona mumbled, but Nafisa ignored her and continued…

"Drive you home safely and give you a hot plate of biryani that Ammi has prepared specially for you."

The mention of Ammi always brought a smile on Sona's lips. Ammi was Nafisa's grandmother. Nafisa lived with her. She had been living with her since she shifted to Mumbai to join College. Her mother and stepfather were in Dubai. She visited them occasionally, but for many years now, Ammi was all the family she had. She was content. Ammi had somehow taken a shine for Sona. "Your little friend", as she referred to her when talking to Nafisa.

As Nafisa parked the car and Sona took out the luggage from it, she saw Ammi coming out of the house. As always, Ammi was immaculately dressed. She wore a pearl-white salwar kameez and a white lace dupatta over her head, her feet were in maroon velvet jootis. She was the epitome of old-world grace. Sona went over to her and touched her feet. "All well beti? How is Rajeev?" Ammi asked.

Cursory questions that needed only mumbled answers...the three of them then entered the house. Ammi had kept tea ready and after drinking a cup of Ammi-brand tea, sweet and milky, Sona felt energised.

"Come, I'll show you your room," Nafisa said, "You freshen yourself up and then come down for lunch."

As the two of them took her stuff upstairs, Sona appreciated anew the old house built by Ammi's father. A pre-Independence structure, it had weathered the storms well and stood solid, proud, aged like a venerable sage amidst the ugly modern buildings surrounding it. The design was old-fashioned. Upstairs was a gallery and three spacious rooms in a row...all with attached bathrooms. The bathrooms were a recent addition, built with the intention of keeping student tenants. But now, Nafisa occupied one room and two rooms were vacant. The room next to Nafisa's would be Sona's. There was a latched connecting door between the rooms. Sona cast an eye over the room. It was neat, and adequately furnished. It was equipped with a comfortable bed, a table and chair, a wardrobe and a window with a view of a large neem tree just outside. What more could a girl ask for in a place like Mumbai where accommodation was unavailable even in exchange of love or lucre?

Sona turned to Nafisa with gratitude and said, "Thank you Nafisa, you are a true friend!"

"Well Sona, I hope you know what you are doing. Mumbai is not the kindest of places. Anyway, you can have this room as long as you want. Take a shower now and we will chat after lunch."

With that, Nafisa swished out of the room and Sona bent down to take her clothes out of the suitcase. Half an hour later she went down cleaned, scrubbed and dressed in a plain mustard cotton salwar-kameez and an elaborately embroidered phulkari dupatta. She helped Nafisa lay the table and the three of them sat down companionably to share the excellent mutton-biryani that was Ammi's speciality. Ammi enquired politely about Sona's mother, husband, house and prospective career plans, but out of some innate courtesy refrained from probing further.

Later, Sona sat in Nafisa's room as Nafisa prepared coffee in the little kitchenette upstairs. "So…" Nafisa said, "Tell me everything!"

Just then Sona's mobile chirped and the screen flashed 'Rajeev'…her heart did a somersault at the sight of the name.

"Hello!" Sona said and Nafisa watched her through lowered lashes. Sona's body language had changed. She sat straightened in her chair now, and spoke in monosyllables.

"Of course," she was saying, "I'll keep in touch. You take care. Call me when you are back in Shivagaon." And she said bye and kept the phone down. The two women looked at each other, the silence between them more evocative than words.

"He knows I'm here. He knows that I will be joining work tomorrow. He has promised to keep me updated. All that remains is to go with the flow," Sona said. She looked out of the window. An ugly black crow was feeding her young in an untidily made nest. "I should call up Mother too. Brief her about this before she gets strange ideas about this move." And Sona picked up the mobile and walked out into the balcony. Talking to Mother needed all her energies and concentration.

When she came back into the room, Nafisa was pouring herself a second cup of coffee and Sona extended her cup as well.

"Now Dr Nafisa Ahmed!" Sona smiled, "Tell me what's new in your life."

Nafisa was a friend that Sona had made in her adult life and so, unlike the case with childhood friends, their friendship had taken time to warm up. It had to go through a long period of formal bowing and scraping before they could reach a comfort level. And even now, given Nafisa's and Sona's rather reserved natures, they were never the chummy, back-slapping, all-hanging-out friends that strong friends are generally expected to be. They had met at a National Conference organised by Delhi University a few years ago. Nafisa was a panellist in the morning session. She was the youngest, brightest and most beautiful panellist and all eyes were turned to her. In her capacity as Press, Sona noticed Nafisa's passion for her subject and her in-depth knowledge of the topic at hand. She had introduced herself to Nafisa during the tea break. She came to know that Nafisa was a Professor at the Political Science Department of Mumbai University. She was single, a few years older than Sona, author of a book and already a member of the Senate at Mumbai University. Sona had felt herself drawn to the quiet strength that Nafisa radiated and the two of them had kept in touch, meeting occasionally, their bond deepening slowly but surely.

When Sona received the appointment letter from Mr Tiwari, the first name that leapt into her mind was that of Nafisa's. Expectedly enough, Nafisa had offered her the room at the top. "As a starting point, this place was not bad," Sona thought. She would soon look for the right PG accommodation closer to her office. But now, the proximity of Ammi, the company of Nafisa and the shelter of this old house wrapped her in a warm blanket of security that she was reluctant to forego. She would talk about her accommodation plans with Ammi at a later stage, when things settled and her mind was at ease.

Sona looked again at Nafisa. She was telling her about an up-coming International Conference to be held in Casablanca, Morocco, where she was to deliver the keynote address.

"I never thought that my second book would make me so famous in academic circles. It was a topic close to my heart, but that it would bring me fame, was something beyond my imagination," Nafisa said.

She had been working on the status of women in the politics of developing economies and the book was the result of all her research and analysis. Sona looked at Nafisa with admiration. She was so young, so beautiful, and except for the scholarly frown-line between her eyebrows, there was nothing of the dry academic about her. Her dress-sense, her speech, her movements, and her voice were understated and substantial. She was a woman of substance. Sona thought of her mother. She thought about her beautiful, authoritative mother, available for the public 24x7... But for her daughter? For her daughter ...so remote and judgmental.

Sona sighed and got up. "You get on with your day Nafisa"; she said, "I'll go and set up my luggage."

4

She kept down the phone and then looked out of the window, seeing with unseeing eyes the wide expanse of lush green lawn. She put up a hand to her brow and rubbed her frown away. What was this girl up to now? Could she not hold on to a single thing and make a success of it? Kamla Pradhan's brow always clouded when she thought of the moves Sona made. Her indecisiveness, her carefree acceptance of life, her unassertiveness in the face of opposition, her go-with-the flow attitude, and her lack of focus, all reminded Kamla of her poor husband. She struggled to draw Sona away from the mistakes her father had made, but the more she pulled Sona, the more the girl wriggled away from her.

Even her decision to marry Rajeev…now that was one point on which Sona had stood very uncharacteristically firm. Though Kamla thought that Sona was marrying in haste, she had allowed the marriage to happen as for the first time she saw a spark of tenacity in Sona. But having married him, she ought to have stuck on in that Shivagaon. Making a home out of that palatial house that Rajeev had built and by becoming an ideal wife, society lady and mother of well-brought up children. But that too the silly girl could not sustain for more than a year. Soon after calling Sona on her first wedding anniversary, Kamla had an inkling of the cracks. Sona had sounded strained and cagey about the happenings of that day. Always a bit reserved with her mother, she had clamped shut whenever the topic of her first wedding anniversary had come up.

And now, she had just called from Mumbai, from her friend Nafisa's home. She informed that she had taken up the job at *News* and now intended to stick on with it come what may! Kamla knew all about Sona's quicksilver change of decisions and plans. As a mother, she would have to make a trip to Mumbai and see that Sona was fine. Sona had expressly forbidden her to come. "But what did the silly girl know about how things worked in India," Kamla thought. She had always led a protected life, cushioned from life's knocks because of her mother's position. Powerful political connections never did harm to anyone in India!

"Sona was one project that," Kamla thought, "I have not succeeded in." Well, she corrected herself, "one can hardly call one's child a project," and yet, the more Kamla succeeded in her public life the less she succeeded in her personal life. She thought of her personal life, she thought about Sona, Mahendra and… and Vikrant.

It had been a shock to see Vikrant that day at the President's 'At Home'. He looked unbelievably handsome in his full military uniform. She had read his name in the list of military officers to be conferred with the Ati Vishisht Seva Medal (AVSM), and had half-expected to meet him. But when she actually came face to face with him, her heart lurched and her stomach became jelly. She told herself, "Impossible to have such feelings for a man after so many years!" She had thought that she was way past such feelings now…hardly a woman in fact…only a public figure.

He had aged well. His salt and pepper hair gave his face a distinguished look. Brig Vikrant Singh had been awarded the AVSM for his tenure in J&K during the worst skirmishes in the valley. He stood there, proud and erect, his charming chiffon and pearl clad wife holding on to his arm. Kamla drifted unobtrusively towards where he stood and as though by some sixth sense, he turned and their eyes met. The crowd melted, the chatter became a soundless music and the two looked at each other as though for eternity.

In fact, it was only for a few seconds and no one saw that strong current of electricity that passed between them. Only his wife guessed. With an intuition that only wives possess, she drew closer to him and held his hand tightly in her grip.

Kamla saw the gesture, smiled inwardly and walked over to them, a formal expression pasted on her face. She greeted them both and Vikrant did the introductions.

"Meet my wife Swaroop, and Swaroop, meet Mrs Kamla Pradhan, Union Minister for Civil Aviation. I think I told you that we knew each other as children."

"Hardly children," Kamla thought, as she recalled Vikrant's physique, tall and strong even at seventeen.

He had been the Sports Captain of the school and she had been the Head Girl. They were classmates and neighbours, a common boundary wall separating the government houses where their families lived. They studied together, laughed together and cycled to school together. From the start they had a strong connection. It was always 'we' and 'us' with them, rarely 'I' and 'you'.

Kamla recalled the summer after the Board Exams. They spent hardly a moment away from each other that summer. They were so perfect for each other that it was impossible to think of a life where the two of them would live apart. The two joined in a perfect circle, like Yin and Yang. The results came… she had topped her school. She took admission in one of the most elite colleges in Delhi University. Vikrant aced his NDA exam and soon packed his bags for Khadakwasla. The two lovers met passionately and tearfully for a last time in his messy room, promising to be always friends, promising to come for each other soon…as soon as their career dreams were attained, as soon as Life and its complications had been taken care of.

Life had other plans though. Student politics swept Kamla away from everything else in the first year of college. She stood for elections in her final year. That she would win was a foregone conclusion. Win she did, and simultaneously the Youth Wing of the Akhil Bharatiya Janhit Party took her in. Soon after joining the Post-Graduate course in Political Science at Delhi University, she was given major responsibilities of the Party. Her two years of MA were a whirl, where she hardly had time to visit her parents in the little railway township that held memories of love and Vikrant. She did very well in her MA and her parents wanted her to take up the scholarship that Oxford was offering her, but in her mind, her future was already chalked out. Her future lay with the Akhil Bharatiya Janhit Party, and she refused the scholarship and plunged full-time into politics.

By then, Vikrant had his commission. He was posted in Aizawl, Mizoram. They met that summer after a long gap. Kamla remembered that day clearly. The day Vikrant had climbed over the boundary wall as usual and met her under the mango trees where she sat on the swing as usual. He had got down on his knee and proposed to her with a simple gold ring. This was a scene that both had known would happen inevitably one day. Her response was unexpected. Looking at the dear face of her lover, she had shaken her head. She refused him because she loved him too much. He deserved a full-time wife, a wife whose only focus in life would be Vikrant, Vikrant, and Vikrant! And she, Kamla, had dedicated herself to a cause. Uplifting the poor, empowering the weak, and enriching the marginalised were her goals and for this, love had to be sacrificed. She thought her heart would break when she saw the hurt and bewilderment in his eyes as he wordlessly took back the ring he had offered her with so much hope. He did not press her again and just turned on his heels and walked away. She sat there, crying great gulps of grief as she watched the mischievous playmate of her childhood and the magical lover of her youth disappear behind the trees. He was taking the sunshine with him, leaving her in shadow.

"Krishna! Krishna!" she called him with the love-name she had given him, but he never turned back and from that day on, Kamla knew that it would be a solitary journey of duty and sacrifice. With a mutual and unspoken agreement, they had deliberately lost touch with each other.

When Kamla gave back Vikrant's ring, it seemed that she gave back her lucky talisman. The aura of good fortune that had surrounded her till then was gone. Her father died soon after, unexpectedly and suddenly of a heart attack and her mother's health took a turn for the worse because of the shock. The Akhil Bharatiya Janhit Party dissolved, destroyed because of internal fights. Vikrant married the daughter of his Commandant, wooed ardently by the old man! He was too good a catch to remain single for long. When Kamla looked at his wedding card, she felt as if a knife had been twisted in her heart. It was around the same time when doctors diagnosed cancer in her mother's stomach. That year… without a job, without a lover, without a vocation…running around trying to arrange funds for her mother's treatment, Kamla knew what hell was in this lifetime itself.

During the final stages of her mother's illness, when both knew that the end was near, the only topic her mother talked about was Kamla's marriage. She wanted to see her daughter married. She did not want her daughter to be alone in this world. Marriage was the last thing on Kamla's mind, but worn down with the constant harping and daily complaints of her mother, she finally allowed her to find her a 'suitable boy.' He was of the same community, four years older than her, employed in a company, came from a respectable family...he would confer on her the status of wife, keep her safe, give her protection and be her companion for life. After Vikrant, Kamla was sure that she would never find real love again. Therefore, it did not matter either way. She said yes. That is how Kamla Vasishtha had become Mrs Kamla Pradhan, submitting herself to matrimony because Life was no longer in her control.

From the start however, it was an unequal marriage. Though Sona was born just a year after the wedding, the child could not seal the bond of love between her parents. Mahendra's constant job-hopping and relocating from place to place convinced Kamla that if she hitched her wagon to his engine, both would fall into a ditch. When Sona turned six and Mahendra started talking of shifting and doing farming in his ancestral village in Ratnagiri District, Kamla finally took the decision of unhooking her wagon from his engine. She found a job as a lecturer in a college in Mumbai and she enrolled Sona in a nearby school.

"You are welcome to go and settle down in that village of yours. But there is no way I am going to jeopardise my daughter's education and future by tagging along there. You can find a good enough job here in Mumbai if you try. The two of us will earn and bring up our daughter together. But I will not accompany you to that village."

Mahendra faded away from their lives then. There was never a formal divorce, but his presence in their lives became lesser and lesser. Kamla had already joined the All India Democratic Party by then, and had become active again in politics, making fast progress up the ladder. Sona was admitted in a boarding school in Panchgani. When news came that Mahendra had died of a heart attack in his village, there was no real pain, only a feeling of regret.

Kamla looked out of the wide window at the immaculately maintained lawn of her appointment bungalow. A gardener was watering the flowerbeds and the garden looked lovely. The journey of becoming the Union Minister for Civil Aviation had been swift and inevitable. When you travel alone, you travel fast. But there was nobody to share the beautiful scene with. Vikrant's face swam into her memory again. She had wanted to share her excitement of seeing him, when she had called Sona up to wish her on her first wedding anniversary. But relations between mother and daughter had never been smooth and comfortable and though she almost blurted out her news to Sona, the girl's cool, almost cold voice over the phone stopped her and she let go the moment. She could not confide in her daughter. She could not share her intimate joys and sorrows with her only child. She was truly alone. If she fell, there would be no one to pick her up. If she soared, there would be no one to share her joyous flight.

5

Sona pushed back her swivel chair and got up when the office boy came and informed her that the Editor wanted to see her. What did the boss want now from her? It was a different environment for Sona this time around. She had completed more than a month in *News* by now but she still felt like an outsider. The relaxed but motivated atmosphere that had been the hallmark of Papa Lobo's regime had been replaced with an atmosphere of petty competitiveness and intrigue. People spied on each other and Tiwari encouraged a culture of sycophancy. He was a very different kettle of fish from Papa Lobo indeed. Papa Lobo had an avuncular, jolly, Santa Claus kind of persona but Tiwari had fish-like eyes that looked at you expressionlessly.

Sona knocked on his door and got prepared to wait. He did that often. He made her wait like an errant schoolgirl visiting the Head Master's office. For some reason he resented the fact that she had been Papa Lobo's protégé and treated her with coolness that was borderline rudeness.

But surprise of surprises! The moment she knocked, Fish-Eyes jumped up and opened the door for her. "Sit down! Sit down!" He said, waving her to a chair. Just as she was wondering what had tamed the ogre, the cat tumbled out of the proverbial bag.

"I just got a call from your mother's Secretary. She will be visiting our office this afternoon, soon after lunch. Why did you not tell me that you are Mrs Kamla Pradhan's daughter? No one in this office mentioned this fact either. Sometimes I feel as if the whole office is in a conspiracy to keep secrets from me. I am a great fan of your mother's you know. One of the best CMs that Maharashtra ever had! And a news agency can always do with political connections."

"So that means this is the end of my ever having to wait at his door," Sona thought, and her jaw clenched.

What a scene it was when Mother finally arrived at the *News* office, with her patrol cars and security in tow. Fish-Eyes was there to open the car door for her and was jumping up and down with excitement. He took her around the newsroom, escorted her around the building and over coffee in his office briefed her about the plans of *News*.

Sona got permission to leave with her mother, as her mother would be departing for Delhi in the evening. As Sona sat in the back seat, squashed between her mother and Mr Venugopal, her Secretary, she felt that she would explode with all the unsaid things that she wanted to throw at her mother, but knowing the futility of it all, she kept quiet. Still, ten minutes into the journey, her patience collapsed and turning a sullen face to her mother she hissed, "I told you not to come, didn't I?"

"And since when are my comings and goings to be dictated by what you say?" her mother countered.

"But Mother…" Sona began passionately, but her mother just put up her hand and Sona sputtered into silence, acutely aware of the perked up ears of Mr Venugopal beside her and the driver and bodyguard sitting in front. Sona had had little privacy in her life with Mother. Mother's political career entailed that there was always a swarm of people around her. Most of Sona's schooling had been in Boarding school. When she came home on holidays, she rarely had her mother to herself. Even if physically mother were with her, mentally and emotionally she would be elsewhere. Sona got this constant feeling that she never was top priority with her mother. When she wanted to share her excitement, sorrow, or apprehension, Mother was never available. With time, Sona learnt to curb her spontaneity with her mother, and now she never counted Mother as her closest confidante. Mother never shared her problems or excitement with her either. Sona turned to look at mother's sharp profile. Difficult to imagine this woman having spurts of joy or sorrow.

Mother was always in control…of the situation, of her emotions, and of life. "Well," Sona thought miserably, "it was high time she learnt that she could not control her daughter's life now. Her daughter was now an adult, who would live life on her terms, encounter her own triumphs and failures and find her own joys and sorrows. She would sail her own boat. She would be the captain of her own ship."

The cars stopped at the Government Guest House where Mother was staying. They all poured out of the vehicles and it was a good one hour later before Sona finally had her mother all to herself. Mother sat regally in the armchair by the window, sipping a tall glass of lime and soda, while Sona paced agitatedly up and down, talking to her in a high-pitched voice that always gave away her disturbed mood.

"I told you Mother not to come down to Mumbai for my sake. Why can't you leave me alone? Do you enjoy creating a scene? Being the centre of attention? I will never be Sona Jayakar in that office now. Always I will be the daughter of the Union Minister for Civil Aviation. I will never know whether a prestigious assignment has come my way because of my own merit or because my mother happens to be the former Chief Minister of Maharashtra."

Her mother let her speak. By the time Sona finished her passionate diatribe, Kamla had finished her tall glass of lime and soda. Then she looked at the young woman who flopped down exhaustedly in the chair opposite and said crisply, "Finished?"

Sona only looked at her, her expression sullen. "Since when did having a parent in power become a disadvantage in India? Learn to enjoy the success of your loved ones Sona, and learn not to be embarrassed with success. Your father never learnt that lesson and I do not want you to repeat his mistakes. This world will excuse anything, *anything*, if you are a success. These are the things that count--- duty, ambition, and success!"

Sona turned to her with a troubled face. "And love Mother?" She asked, "Does love not count? And happiness?"

Mother looked at her with an inscrutable expression. "Love? Happiness?" she said softly, "They are fickle companions, meant for the ordinary. If you want to touch the sky, then you will have to rise above these petty pursuits of common folk. Duty! Duty should always be paramount."

6

It was a Sunday like any other Sunday. But it was different and special because it was a Sunday in Ammi's house. Ammi was crocheting an elaborate white tablecloth as a gift for her cousin's daughter who was getting married next month. Nafisa was reading a book and Sona was painting her toenails red. These calm Sunday mornings in Ammi's house recharged her batteries for the week. Rising without hurry, doing her yoga exercises (suryanamaskars and pranayama), massaging her head with hot oil, eating two of Ammi's alu paranthas with a bowl of dahi, taking a leisurely shower, completing some pending work...Today's pending work was doing pedicure and manicure. She was going out for dinner with Shubhendu tonight and needed to do some urgent beauty maintenance---something about which she was always lazy and tardy. As she watched the bold red colour bring life back to her freshly groomed feet, she sighed with happiness. She chuckled when she remembered what Shubhendu had said when she had described her Sunday routine to him. "Idyllic Female Paradise!" he had said.

Nafisa looked up from her book. "What?!"

Sona told her about the conversation. Nafisa put

down her book. "This Shubhendu," she said softly, "You confide in him a lot, is it? And why should you be discussing our routine with him?"

Sona looked up from her nail painting. "Oh he is just a colleague Nafisa. We work on assignments together. He is quite senior to me...Age-wise…and professionally too. I learn a lot from him. Besides, he is lonely. He needs a shoulder to lean on. I seem to be that shoulder."

Nafisa looked quizzical.

"His wife left him for his best friend some six months ago. He has still not recovered. Some women, I tell you! You know, she and that beau of hers used to carry on shamelessly right in front of his eyes!"

"And Shubhendu babu used to just gaze lovingly at them?"

"What else could he do? He is a straightforward man, a gentleman. He could not have challenged that guy to a duel. He just waited for their passion to cool. He did not want his marriage to break up. Though there are no children involved, he loved that woman! But some women just don't deserve decent men! I hope that lover of hers ditches her soon!"

"And Shubhendu babu sits and bitches to you about his wife, a runaway wife!"

"Oh Nafisa! Do not say that he 'bitches'! That is a harsh word and sexist too! He just confides in me. It lightens his burden. Sharing your worries and sorrows with somebody helps you heal faster."

"Just be careful Sona! He is trying to snare you! Men who complain about their wives to other women are trying to hook them. And you darling, are soooo hookable! With your innocent, little-girl-lost look and your hurt eyes…"

Sona giggled, "My dear Nafisa. Thanks for worrying! But I'm hardly a babe-in-the-woods that you are painting me out to be! I am a big girl now, with a husband, home and hearth of my own! And why would Shubhendu want to take advantage of me! What do I have to offer?"

Nafisa gave her then a look that made Sona flush. "Oh forget it Nafisa!" she said with a dismissive wave of her hand. "Leave poor Shubhendu Roy alone! We are just colleagues who happen to be friends. Topic closed."

Nafisa gave a shrug and went back to her book.

As Sona dreamily turned the lid on the nail-polish bottle, she recalled that sultry afternoon of a few weeks back. Shubhendu and she had decided to check out the new Art and Book exhibition held at Kala Ghoda. As she waited for him to arrive at the appointed spot, she checked out her surroundings. She noticed that near the bookstall, a book reading was happening. At the other end, arrangements for the tabla recital in the evening were in progress. Under another colourful pandal, a painting exhibition was on. She watched the arty-looking crowd, fashionably careless in dress and attitude, come and go, talking of T S Eliot…and of course, Michelangelo! Then she turned and saw

Shubhendu, hurrying towards where she stood. There was a spring in his step today as he jumped over a rope banister and came to her with a boyish smile on his face. "Sorry for keeping you waiting", he huffed, "Let's go! But before that…" He took out a pen-drive and said, "Julio Iglesias collection."

"How sweet! How did you know that I love him?"

"I figured that we'd have the same taste!"

The little pink pen-drive with a pink ribbon tied at its loop winked in the sun. It exchanged hands. She looked at him, kissed the pen-drive and put it in her jeans pocket.

They spent a wonderful two hours at the exhibition, picking up books, looking at paintings, sharing nuts from one cone, having hot tea. They had the same taste not only in music but also in books and films. They discussed non-stop the films they had seen, the books they had read, the assignments they had worked on together and the colleagues who needed to be put in place. They stopped at a sandwich kiosk for a quick bite and it was then, between big mouthfuls of cheese and lettuce and bread that he asked her if she would come and spend the next Sunday at his pad.

"Oh no! Never on a Sunday!" She said laughing. He asked her why and she told him about her Sunday ritual at Ammi's house. "Sunday mornings are sacrosanct!" she said, "I am so lucky to have Ammi and Nafisa in my life. You have to eat Ammi's biryani. It is so yummy! And Nafisa! You have to meet her to know what a gem she is!"

"If this Nafisa is as wonderful as you say she is, how come she is still not married?"

"Oh, come on Shubhendu! I did not expect this from you! Not everything in a woman's life centres on marriage. Maybe she has not found the right person yet. And maybe she is happy as she is, with Ammi, and now, with me!"

"Hmmm…" He looked at her thoughtfully, "Idyllic Female Paradise!"

"Yes! And don't *you* be the snake that disrupts it!"

As they browsed through a stall of technology books, she spotted a red covered book on motorcycles. Rajeev loved motorcycles. This was just the book for him! She picked it up and looked at the pictures inside. She had called him up before he left for Singapore. It was nine in the night. He was still in the factory. "Go home now Rajeev," she told him, "You'll kill yourself with too much work."

"Hmm," he said, "Nobody waiting for me there." She had sensed the unspoken accusation in his voice. That was partly the reason why she avoided calling him too often. He always sent her on a guilt trip, without explicitly saying anything. He put on this wonderful mask of what an understanding and liberal husband he was. How he had 'allowed' her to stay away from her marital home so that she could further her career ambitions. How generous and forgiving he was, as he took care of all her monthly expenses. How dutiful a husband he was as he never complained about the domestic discomforts he may have to encounter at home. But underneath it all, lay that needle of accusation that pricked her and made her bleed each time she spoke to him. She refrained from sharing with him her little triumphs and successes at work. Slowly, she stopped telling him of her troubles as well. He was financially generous, never demanding an explanation of her expenses and giving her free and unlimited access to his Visa card. But it was also true that he did this because he had full faith that she would never misuse this privilege. Of the two, she was the stingier partner. Once her salary started, she rarely used Rajeev's Visa card. She spent little on clothes or cosmetics. Her major expenses included money spent on commuting and the monthly rent. She had now officially become Ammi's PG, forcing Ammi to accept the amount that she used to get from her earlier tenants. But Sona knew that Ammi's tasty food and loving care and Nafisa's company and friendship were priceless gifts that could never be compensated by cash alone.

Sona scanned the title of the bright red book ---- *Motorcycles: Yesterday and Today.* She turned the book, weighed it in her hands and slowly put it back. She moved on to the next table but as she moved away, she sighted through the corner of her eyes, a long-haired, bearded guy in slouchy jeans pick up the book she had just kept down. He scanned the book, looked at the front cover, turned it, looked at the price, and then shaking his head, returned it to its place. As he moved away, Sona hurried to the table and grabbed the book into her hands. This was Rajeev's book. And he would have it!

As Sona picked up the pedicure paraphernalia and went up to her room, she saw the yellow packet. The packet in which the red-covered book lay, waiting to be read and fingered by Rajeev.

Just a day after the outing with Shubhendu, Rajeev had called and said that he was going for two weeks to Singapore on work. "Two weeks?" Sona had exclaimed and Rajeev said that he was going to attend a short workshop while meeting some clients based in Singapore. It was to be a two-week work-cum-study tour. After that day, there had been no calls and Sona too had not tried to contact him. She wondered about the workshop, "What is the workshop for?" She wished that he would confide in her a little and discuss the issues of his work with her. True, she would not understand the intricacies, but at least he could explain in layman's language. If he was going on a study cum work visit, then he needed his secretary with him, the indispensable and trustworthy Preeti. Preeti was the confidante who understood the pressures of his job, the loyal subordinate who always stood by him. As Sona stood by the window, looking at the silent nest of the crow in the neem tree, she saw in her mind's eye the short and chubby Preeti bending down to hand over a paper to Rajeev as he talked with his Chinese clients. She saw clearly the upward curve of his lips as he smiled and took the paper from her hands and the dimples that appeared on Preeti's smooth cheeks as her eyes met his. Sona dug her fingers into her palm and felt as though her body was on fire. "That unfaithful husband of hers and that scheming little gold-digger!" She thought. She felt that her head would burst with jealousy. If Rajeev had come in front of her at this moment, she would have shot him without a thought.

7

It was Sunday again. Rajeev wished that there never were Sundays. He was at a loss on Sundays. He suffered from withdrawal symptoms whenever he was away from work. After Sona left, Sundays were truly pathetic. Yes, Rajeev felt abandoned and very sorry for himself. This was the truth and he had better learn to face it. His wife had left him, maybe not legally, but physically and emotionally, she had drifted away. But why? How? Rajeev was truly flummoxed. He had denied her nothing. Her complaint was that he was wedded to his job. But he was working for her sake. Every wife wanted her husband to be a success. One had to work hard to be a success. But Sona never could understand his passion for his work. She treated *Geeta Engineering Works* more as a mistress than as her husband's career. She never tried to understand the pressures of his work, never showed any interest in the workings of the factory. "Your factory!" she said, "Your work!"

"Our factory!" He would correct her, "Our work!"

But she would only shake her pretty head and say, "I come second Rajeev, in your list of priorities. That factory will always be your first love."

"Well, the factory was conceived before you came. It is dear to me, but so are you!"

Geeta Engineering Works was his gift to his mother. He had named it after the woman who brought him and his brother up. He had started taking care of himself at a very young age, and had felt, as soon as he finished school, deeply responsible for his mother. He wanted to wipe out that hurt and bewildered look from her face and had vowed very early in life to become a very rich and successful man and give to his mother all the luxuries that fate had snatched away from her and that were hers by right. She was not designed to lead a single life, not designed to take decisions on her own, not designed for widowhood. Rajeev had grown up feeling responsible for his mother, then feeling responsible for his business, then feeling responsible for the welfare of all his employees and finally feeling responsible for Sona. He was only in his thirties, but felt much older.

He knew his father only as a framed photo hung on his mother's bedroom wall--- Maj. Raghav Jayakar, who never aged. His handsome but stern visage had followed Rajeev throughout his growing up years. He was less a father and more a legend. He could never forgive his father for dying so young and leaving his wife, helpless as a sparrow, vulnerable as a butterfly, to cope alone with the knocks of life. As the years passed and his beloved mother aged, adding silver to her fine hair, her husband looked down at them all, smiling, smiling. His mother had loved the man, loved him still. She never looked at another man. She moved back to her father's home and Rajeev's maternal grandfather was the only father figure in his life.

"Never forget that your father was a war hero", their mother said repeatedly, "Never do anything that would disappoint his memory."

Meanwhile they struggled on. Rajeev, his elder brother Arjun and their delicate bird-like mother were surviving on the military pension, which their mother received. Arjun was older by five years. He was brilliant in studies and excellent in sports. He won a scholarship to an American University soon after his graduation. Two years later, he was sending home cheques that made him the man of the family. Rajeev watched with envy the expression of adoration in his mother's eyes when Arjun came home for the first time from the US. He married young. He married the girl his mother chose. She was the daughter of a wealthy man. This alliance catapulted them into a different social sphere. He went back to the US with his wife. A year later he called his mother to live with them. That is where she stayed, the Geeta of *Geeta Engineering Works*. "Come and stay with me!" Rajeev pleaded.

"I'll come"; his lovely mother had told him, "I'll come when you give me news of the arrival of your first child."

But now, circumstances being what they were, a child, a family life, domestic bliss---all seemed a remote possibility. He had fallen for Sona because she looked so vulnerable, so lost, so in need of protection. Who would have thought that she would turn out to be so headstrong?

He remembered the picnic with Monica and

Shaan. He had seen Sona before, in get-togethers and parties, as they happened to have common friends. But it was in this picnic that he noticed her delicate and dark beauty. She was wearing a simple white top and blue jeans.

She used to wear simple clothes those days. It was only lately that she had taken to wearing heavy ethnic Indian dresses and saris. Her taste in clothes had gone from understated Western chic to heavy ethnic. He failed to understand why. She had looked so charming that day of the picnic. As they sat cross-legged on the rug by the riverside, he engineered to sit by her, their knees touching. She hardly looked at him, and he saw only her fine profile. Her diamond stud sparkled suddenly in the sun. She was ignoring him. She did not laugh at his jokes, did not make eye contact, kept a physical distance... she intrigued him. He, Rajeev Jayakar was not used to being ignored. They had all then decided to cross the little river to the other side. Sona was the tiniest of them all, and Rajeev was the tallest. The water came up to her waist and she was scared to go further. Monica and Shaan, both strapping and tall, strode forward. Rajeev gave Sona his hand and she held on tight as he guided her through the swift current to the other side. She had looked at him then and smiled. Her charming smile captured his heart. Shaan had clicked his camera and captured that moment forever. It was Sona's favourite snap and she had framed it and put it on their bedside table.

It was after that picnic that they had started meeting each other, separately from the group.

Although in the earlier days, it was he who plotted their rendezvous, as the days progressed, it was Sona who always took the lead. He was living on his own, but Sona had to get past her mother at home. Rajeev did not know why Mrs Kamla Pradhan resented him. The distrust was mutual anyway. He never developed a rapport with the strong personality that was Sona's mother.

"Don't mind her", Sona had told him, "Mother would have hated anyone who was taking her daughter away from her strong clutches. Do not feel bad if she does not love you. Mother loves no one. She is entirely self-absorbed. I do not think she even knows the meaning of love. She never loved my father you know. She neglected him when he needed her most. 'Love' is an alien word in Mother's dictionary."

He was working with a multinational at that time but already the idea of *Geeta Engineering Works* had taken root. He worked in his office in the daytime and at night worked on his proposal for *Geeta Engineering Works*. Then Sona happened. She was a sweet distraction. The girl he did not want to let go. The girl with the vulnerable eyes. The girl who always looked as though she wanted to be at some other place.

He put aside *Geeta Engineering Works* for a while and concentrated on Sona. He wooed her with the same precision and concentration that he brought to all that he pursued.

Rajeev ran a hand over his face. He had not thought that life would take this unexpected turn. He had ticked all the 'must do' boxes of life.

He studied hard, got into IIT, landed a good job and married a pretty girl of a prominent politician. Till that point, he was on par with Arjun. He had now hoped to tick the remaining boxes, with two beautiful children, and a successful business. Then, his mother would come and live with him. But this hasty departure of Sona's, this quirk of hers to work when there was no financial need for it…Rajeev brushed a lock of hair away from his forehead with frustration. He picked up his cup of tea and looked at the spacious hall of his house. It was beautifully decorated. He had called an interior designer to do up the interiors of his house a few months before his marriage. Sona got a ready-made, fully decorated house when she came as a new bride. How many brides could boast of that? He looked at the hall, but something was missing. It lacked soul. He got up and walked around the exquisite furniture.

What was missing? And then, it struck him. Those flower decorations that Sona used to do. The hall used to have at least five glass vases with flowers in them when she was around. She was so clever that she could make a pretty arrangement even with just leaves and twigs. Yes, he missed the flower arrangements. The Sona-touch to his house.

He came out to the garden, to where Dara sat regally. She would be back, he thought to himself. But maybe, she won't be. He had felt her withdrawal from the day of their disastrous first wedding anniversary.

He re-lived that awful day again in his mind. He had wrapped up his work quickly and was about to call it a day, when he got a panic call from Security. There was a fire in one of the godowns. He had rushed out of office and when he saw the flames leaping out from the godown, it was as though his own body was on fire. Crazed with fear and apprehension, he had run around, arranging for the fire brigade, the fire control apparatus of his own factory premises, marshalling his employees together for damage control, putting on a brave front for the sake of his frightened employees.

In all this frenzy, he completely forgot to call up Sona. He saw the two missed calls from home on his mobile when he climbed into his car well past midnight. He drove fast and his heart plunged when he saw the house and the garden wrapped in darkness. With a feeling of foreboding, he ran to the front door. It was open. Where was Dara? Where was Sona? He put on the light in the hall and saw her then. She was sprawled on the floor, with her arms around Dara, fast asleep and dead drunk. That is how he found his exquisite Sona, when he came home that fateful night, dishevelled and dirty.

8

She was driving her sleek black Honda City away from the metropolis. She drove fast and with pleasure. It was pleasure mixed with apprehension. As she left the familiar landmarks of Delhi behind and the typical scenery of rural Haryana emerged, she slowed down a little and began looking for the landmarks that would take her to the little hotel tucked away from prying eyes. Yes, there was that village school from where she had to turn in. She turned left in a cloud of dust and the narrow road started climbing up. This road ended at the hotel. She turned inside the gate and parked her car. She walked into the dimly lit lobby and saw him coming down the stairs. She walked up to him and together they climbed up the stairs, shoulder to shoulder, without speaking. He opened the door of his room and she entered. As soon as the door closed, they were in each other's arms. They were kissing each other as if they had never been away, as if the long intervening years had never encroached.

"Kamla, Kamla!" he whispered in her ear, as he carried her to the big bed in the room, his voice thick with desire, "Why did you go away from me?"

They undressed each other hurriedly, making love urgently and hungrily, as though Time would come and drag them from each other again. Later, he stroked her hair away from her forehead. "You've got silver in your hair. But you are still my beautiful Kamla. Mine!"

She smiled, fingered his cleft chin, and said, "And you, Brig Vikrant Singh, look good in your salt and pepper hair. But you are still my Krishna. Mine!"

They never left the room, ordering in dinner and telling each other of the years lost in-between. As she sat with her head on his shoulder, their hands clasped tightly, she asked him about his life.

Swaroop was the ideal Army wife. She was trained well by her mother, who was herself a General's wife. Swaroop's own background had prepared her for the inevitabilities and unexpectedness of Army life. She enjoyed each and every peace posting and lived uncomplainingly during the field postings, immersing herself whole-heartedly in the cantonment functions and her children's lives. She dressed smartly, was discreet in speech, and prioritised her husband's career above everything else. She threw elegant parties, kept a beautiful home and brought up well-mannered children. Swaroop was all that an ideal wife should be, an ideal wife of an Army officer on the way up.

"Soooo…good!" Kamla said, "It is Vikrant! Vikrant! Vikrant for Swaroop. You've got a loving full-time wife, as I said you deserved."

"Darling," Vikrant said and kissed her hand, "Swaroop loves no one. She is entirely self-absorbed. She does her duty wonderfully though. I cannot fault her on that."

Kamla turned to look at him and Vikrant gave a woeful shrug. They hardly slept that night, talking well into the wee hours, making love slowly and less frantically the second time around---giving and taking and rolling up pleasure in a tight ball. He wrapped his arms protectively around her and asked her about Sona. She confided to him her fears about her and about the distance that was growing ever wider between them.

"Let her loose," he said, "Allow her to be the person she wants to be."

"And suppose she never comes back?"

"She will. Trust me."

As night faded and day broke, they came together one last time. Later he rolled away from her and lay on his back, looking at the ceiling. "Kamla" he said in a gruff voice, "This should never happen again. You know that don't you?"

She looked at him quickly with surprised eyes. "Why?" Her voice was small and frightened.

"Because of who you are and who I am."

"I am ready to give it up for you Vikrant."

He turned on his side and looked at her. "You will sacrifice your duty for me? Those many years ago, when it mattered so much, when we were young and hopeful, you gave me up for your duty."

She looked down.

He put his hand to her cheek. "There are other people involved", he said softly, "I cannot hurt Swaroop. She is very sensitive. It is my duty as a husband to protect her, not hurt her."

She got up from bed then in one swift movement. She went into the bathroom and freshened herself. Brooding, he lay in bed and watched her dress. In a matter of minutes she draped her white cotton sari around her in the style that made the media persons call her the Indira Gandhi of the All India Democratic Party. She picked up her bag and came to where Vikrant lay... his face sad. She bent down and kissed him on the forehead, wrapping him achingly in her lovely perfume. "You are right Vikrant. Duty should always come first."

She was gone then... leaving only her scent behind...and memories... moments... and...and Love!

9

The Singapore flight arrived at ten in the morning at the International Airport in Mumbai. His driver was waiting for him at the airport. Rajeev wanted to be in Shivagaon by evening, so that he could be in office at eight sharp the next morning after a refreshing night's sleep. As the driver negotiated his way out of the tricky parking area, Rajeev looked at the teeming metropolis, throbbing with energy and greed. So, this was where Sona had opted to live! She preferred *this* to the calm peace of Shivagaon. She must be in office now. What was going on with her? He had tried calling her from Singapore, but she never picked up his calls. Finally, he had sent her an e-mail and had received a cryptic reply: "Busy. Working on a deadline. Stressed!" That's all! On an impulse, he leaned forward and told the driver to turn the car towards the *News* office.

The receptionist asked him to take a seat as she spoke on the intercom. Ignoring her, he kept standing. He turned to look in through the glass partition that separated the work area of *News* from the reception section. The place was buzzing with activity like a beehive. People were hurrying from one desk to another, most were typing away fast on their computers and some others were speaking with each other, the gleam of urgency bright in their eyes. Where was Sona? His eyes swept the room from one end to the other looking for her familiar petite figure clad in her favourite ethnic salwar-kameez. Despite scanning the room twice, he was unable to spot her. He looked more carefully again and saw her suddenly. He had seen her the first time but had not recognised her. She looked different. She was dressed in dark blue jeans and a white shirt, topped with an orange-brown short sleeveless jacket. She was wearing black-framed glasses and was talking to a middle-aged fellow, who was leaning rather familiarly on her desk. She looked different. She looked alive. She seemed so at home with her surroundings. He looked at her for long. This was the first time he was seeing her at work. This was *his* Sona, but it was also somebody different. For the first time he looked at her as a separate entity, as a person and an individual with her own identity. She looked happy. It struck him then that he was not the sole provider of her happiness. In his capacity as husband, he need not bring her happiness in little shopping bags. He needed to leave her alone to find her happiness on her own. He turned away, a thoughtful look on his face. He walked out of the reception area even as the receptionist called after him. He came out of the building and called his driver on the mobile. As his car stopped in the porch and he was about to get in, the doors of *News* opened and Sona rushed out, looking from left to right...looking for someone... As soon as she saw him, she hurried up to him. "You were going away without seeing me? The receptionist gave me the message. I was just closing an important file on the computer."

"I could see you were busy…I did not want to disturb you."

"Don't be silly Rajeev. What is your plan for the day?"

Rajeev thought fast, "I've just arrived from Singapore. I am checking into a hotel for the night."

Sona thought fast, "Ok. I will take the day off after lunch. I'll join you there."

They looked at each other for a moment and then smiled at a remembered memory.

When she walked back into office, there was an upward curve to her lips. Shubhendu, who was shuffling some papers at her desk, raised an eyebrow. "You look like a cat, after it has licked the proverbial bowl of cream."

She leaned close to his ear, "Meeeeooow! I'll need your help today Shubhendu. I need to get off work after lunch. I owe you this one." She looked at him with her big, innocent eyes.

The driver came to pick her up during lunch hour. She joined Rajeev in the hotel restaurant. They looked at the menu together and gave their order. Rajeev leaned back then and smiled at her. "This reminds me of our courtship days. When you used to quit early from work and meet me."

She was quiet for a while. Then she asked, "How was your Singapore trip? Did Preeti go back to Shivagaon?"

"Preeti?" He raised his eyebrows. "What made you think that she was in Singapore? I went alone."

After lunch, they went to Ammi's place. There, she gave him the red-covered book on motorcycles. Ammi was overjoyed on meeting Rajeev. She had met him only during their wedding and had liked him instantly. Nafisa was back by teatime. They sat in Ammi's big hall, watching TV, sipping tea, chatting. Rajeev put on the news on TV. Three more police officers had been killed by Chibba, by the dreaded terrorist, who ran a parallel government in the heart of Punjab. The PM was inaugurating the Trade Fair in Delhi. The Union Sports Minister was giving away prizes at the National Games in Chandigarh. A function was taking place at the Maurya Sheraton to commemorate World Tourism Day. There were important dignitaries seated on the dais. The camera hovered indecisively and then finally settled on the aquiline profile of the Union Minister for Civil Aviation. Sona could not suppress a smile. Mother is always the centre of attention, always!

Rajeev reclined in his chair and observed Sona sitting between Ammi and Nafisa, talking animatedly and laughing. Ammi prepared her trademark biryani for dinner in honour of Rajeev. Later the three youngsters strolled out to the corner shop for after-dinner ice cream.

After a long time, Rajeev felt carefree and young. Strolling in the darkened lane of Ammi's quiet neighbourhood, licking his vanilla-flavoured ice cream cone and listening to the chatter of Nafisa and

Sona, he regressed into childhood. His grandfather would sometimes take him and Arjun for after-dinner ice cream on hot summer nights. The three of them would sit on a bench by the road and chatter aimlessly. Rajeev allowed the years to drop off him like water off a duck's back. He missed his grandfather. He was a grand old man who brought up the two boys with good old-fashioned values.

Values that were simple and clear-cut. Parents had to be strict and protective of their children. The children in turn had to be respectful and dutiful towards their parents. The womenfolk had to defer to the men in their lives. The men had to protect and take care of the women in their lives---mother, sister, wife, and daughter. Rajeev's values were his grandfather's values, but seeing Sona today had left him a bit perplexed. It made him realise suddenly that she was quite capable of taking care of herself. He felt cheated somehow, but paradoxically, he also felt relieved.

Finally, he never went back to his hotel for the night. He spent it in Sona's room. He looked around at the hostel-like sparseness of the furnishings. The table and chair by the window, the cupboard, the single bed. Nafisa had given a sleeping bag for him, but he squeezed into the narrow bed along with Sona and they spent the night giggling and whispering and making furtive love, acutely alive to the creaking of the virginal bed and the presence of Nafisa on the other side of the latched door.

10

Sona rushed into the room with a sheaf of papers, and noticed that Mabel and Sudhakar, who were whispering to each other, immediately clamped shut. This happened frequently nowadays. She was now the blue-eyed girl of Fish-Eyes. This did not exactly lead her up the popularity chart with her colleagues. Sona tossed her head. She was not here to win a popularity contest. She was here to work, and become successful. Mother was right, as always. Success put a lid on many faults.

"So…" she turned to Mabel and Sudhakar, "What is the latest buzz?"

"You'd be the first to know that, wouldn't you?" Mabel said with a toothy, false smile, "You are the one who gets all the plum assignments. Wish I had a pretty smile too to help me along."

"Wish I too had a mother in Parliament to help me on," Sudhakar said.

"Mabel", Sona hissed, "We may have joined together this time around, but don't forget that I have more experience than you babies. I was here during Papa Lobo's time too. And Sudhakar, I'd give up wearing white sneakers with black pants if I were you. That would help your career a lot more than a mother in Parliament!" With that, Sona turned briskly and walked out of the room.

Slowly, she had learnt to handle the hidden and not-so-hidden jealousy of her colleagues. Nobody loves a person who is on the way up. Last month's office Diwali party had only added to the hostilities. At the party, it was not her fault that old Mr Prabhu came and chatted with her for such a long time. . Prabhu was the owner and proprietor of Swan Publishing, the media house of which *News* was a part. Sarita told her later that the cats in the office were gossiping that any man, old or young, would chat for a long time when the woman sitting opposite was wearing such a low-cut blouse and a transparent sari! Her cheeks burnt! Sona flushed at the insinuations. As far as she thought, it was a decent blouse and not such a transparent sari!

She went back to her desk and started proofreading the latest article that she and Shubhendu had worked on. Just then, she got a call on the intercom from the Editor's office. Fish-Eyes wanted to see her urgently. She walked up to his cabin, knocked and entered. The days of waiting by the door were long over. Fish-Eyes was scanning something on his computer with suppressed excitement. He had a proposal for her. He wanted her to go and interview Chibba! Chibba had sent him a feeler that he would give one interview, only one, to the mainstream media, and he had chosen *News* for that interview. An explosive interview! "It is a very important, very sensitive interview Sona," he said, "It is also very dangerous. You can refuse if you do not want to go. You will of course have Shubhendu with you on the field. I will not send you alone. But I want you to do the interview. You have that vulnerable and innocent look that can melt the heart of any hardened criminal."

"I'll do it!" Sona said like a shot, "But I have a condition…" Mr Tiwari gave her a look. "A request…" she said hurriedly.

He raised his eyebrows.

"I'll go alone. I want to handle this alone."

Mr Tiwari looked at her silently for some time. Then he smiled. "You know Sona", he said, "You remind me of how I was when I had just started in my career. You have the same fire! All right! You will go alone. You know the risks. You have to be very careful."

Sona came out of the Editor's office with a dazed look in her eyes. This interview would take her career to another level. Shubhendu waved to her from his cubicle. She hurriedly averted her eyes and headed to her desk.

She came home late that evening. Ammi was already asleep. Sona heated the food that was in the fridge and ate absently, all the while thinking of the impending visit to Chibba's heartland. When she went up to her room, she saw the sliver of light from Nafisa's room that indicated that she was still up. But Sona was tired tonight, so she went straight to her room, changed and got into bed with a book. Just as she was thinking that it was time to turn in, there was a knock on the door. Sona opened the door to Nafisa, who came in billowing in her white, kaftan-like nightie and sat down like an ethereal fairy on the chair by the desk. Nafisa was always like this. She gave a 'touch-me-not' vibe. She would have never sat on the bed. Sona looked at Nafisa's virginal face, observing her pale beauty, her classic features, and her Madonna-like expression. Nafisa was telling her about her day, but Sona was only half-listening. She was gazing at Nafisa's face, innocent as a schoolgirl's, guile-less and open like an angel's. "Why is it that such beautiful people are left alone in this world?" thought Sona.

"Why aren't you married Nafisa?" Sona asked suddenly. Coming out like this, the question sounded rude and intrusive. Nafisa was stopped mid-track in her ramblings with the abrupt question. "I...I..." she stammered.

"Sorry;" Sona said shame-faced, "It is none of my business!" Sona noticed Nafisa's downcast expression and cursed herself for her insensitivity.

"No, don't be sorry. You are my closest friend. You can say what you want. I... I.." Nafisa stuttered to a stop.

Sona thought that she should tell Nafisa about the Chibba assignment, but then on second thoughts kept quiet. There were lot of things that Sona did not share with others these days. It made her shoulders droop and her heart heavy with the entire burden.

11

She got off at the railway station, adjusted her backpack and looked around. According to the instructions, she had to come out of the station and take the bus going to Jaswala village. She was to get off at the third stop, in village Kupran, walk towards the abandoned well and wait for her pick-up. It all sounded unnecessarily cloak-and-dagger, but she was not about to show any stupid bravado to people who carried pistols tucked in their socks and revolvers tucked in their belts. Sona had read up on Chibba beforehand and knew that he was riding a tiger. He could not now get off. He carried a massive reward on his head. The police were just waiting to snap him and he was wary of all strangers. He trusted no one. He slept with a gun under his pillow, his eyes opened at the slightest creak and his finger was always on the trigger. She was going to meet this man! Nevertheless, he needed this interview as much as she needed it. The media fed off people like him and he needed the Press to take his voice to the world. He felt that the National mainstream media was projecting him in a wrong light, painting him to be a villain and monster that he was not. He liked to think of himself as a modern Robin Hood, robbing the rich to feed the poor. In these interior parts of the State, Chibba's word was law. He ran a parallel government and the villagers seemed to prefer his anarchy to the corruption of the State.

Sona adjusted the dupatta over her head, and scanned the deserted road once more. She could not see a speck of life. She stood alone in the wilderness, as though she was the last human standing in a lonely planet. Then suddenly, when apprehension had started taking the better of her, a white SUV came onto the main road from an inside lane. Sona's heart beat fast and she clenched her fist tight. The SUV stopped in front of her. Two men got off, one of them tied a blindfold on her eyes and the other took her backpack. They quickly body-searched her. Then they shoved her into the car and the driver started the car. After a few minutes of silence, the man on her right told her that they were driving to Chibba's hideout. It would take half an hour at least. "Thank you for the cordial reception", Sona joked, trying to lighten the atmosphere, but when there was no response from either men on her sides, she clamped shut. It was better not joke with these men, who carried guns in their belts and suspicion in their minds! Because of her blindfold, she could not even read their expressions. The silence was oppressive, and her heart was thudding fast. After driving for approximately fifteen minutes on tarred roads, the car turned left and from the bumps and the jolts, Sona guessed that it was a kaccha road. They were approaching their destination bumpily but surely! After what seemed like an endless drive, the car came to a stop. The man on her left helped her out and then walked her inside a house. She heard the door shut behind her. Someone came and removed her blindfold. She blinked hard even in the darkened room, her eyes getting used to light. Her eyes swept the room and she spied a man sitting on a carpet, which was on a raised platform. His king-like pose reminded her somehow of pictures of Maharaja Ranjit Singh that she had seen in books. He had a flowing black beard, a blue turban and piercing black eyes, which even now were looking at her shrewdly. So this was Chibba! The man who thought himself to be king! Sona joined her hands in a Namaste and bowed. He joined his hands too and waved her to a chair placed near him.

Sona had already prepared her questionnaire in her mind and was going to use the interview technique that she had learnt from Shubhendu. She would not consult a paper. She would just converse with him as though they were chatting at a jolly tea party. She would ask him about his childhood, his youth, and show no interest whatsoever in his political agenda. "That would come inevitably," Shubhendu used to tell her. Never start the interview with questions whose answers you have actually come for. Sona had worked on many assignments with Shubhendu. She knew the truth and effectiveness of this technique.

She gave the bearded man a small smile. He looked in his forties. His sharp nose, his piercing eyes, his turban, and his posture, all gave him a regal stature. It was impossible to be unimpressed by his personality. She cleared her throat and began.

He was the son of gallantry award winner Havildar Gurdiyal Singh. As a mark of respect, villagers of his hometown celebrated his father's birthday as 'Shaheed Din'. But this brave soldier was in his personal life a cruel and violent man, who beat his wife and children. Chibba did not have a single tender memory of his father and when this man raised his hand on his beloved mother, the only overwhelming feeling that arose in the little boy's heart was to silence this father forever. When Chibba heard about his father's death during combat operations, while displaying extraordinary bravery in the line of duty, there was only relief in his mind. He grew up with a hatred of all authority, all father figures, all symbols of State, and all instruments of oppression. He hated all politicians. As he grew older, honing the brave leadership streak that he had inherited from his father, the hatred of mainstream politics and politicians only grew stronger. He was a soldier's son and grandson of a farmer and his sympathies lay strongly with the poor peasants. He felt enraged at the wealthy farmers and the machinations of the State that exploited these peasants. He controlled the area that he called his 'ilaqa' and dispensed there his own brand of rough and tough justice. But he was getting disturbed by the way he was being projected on National TV. "I am not a terrorist. I am fairer than the State. You can ask any poor farmer who he trusts --- the government or Chibba--- and he will say Chibba. People should know my side of the story too. It cannot be all one-sided reportage." Sona nodded sympathetically and Chibba continued talking…

Around lunchtime, they were brought huge thalis of good, wholesome rural fare and like a good host, Chibba urged her to eat more. She saw no signs of the gun that he was supposed to carry at all times, but she did not let down her guard for one moment. Looking at her wary eyes, Chibba assured her of her safety and urged her to let go of fear. He admired her bravery and said that he had never expected a woman journalist. When the interview was over, he even agreed to pose for a photograph and looked the camera straight in the eye in his regal pose. As she packed her camera and other paraphernalia for her journey back, he came and personally tied the blindfold for her almost tenderly, calling her 'Sister'. As he spoke to her in his deep voice, tied the blindfold, and held her shoulders for a moment, she could understand why so many people acknowledged him as their leader. She felt safe with him, not threatened. "You need not be afraid of me," he said, "You are only a messenger who will take my voice to the outside world." With that he released her and the two earlier gentlemen marched her back to the car that was waiting outside.

They made the journey through the same terrain. Sona's senses were alive to the jerks and sounds. Half an hour later, they hauled her out of the car. She staggered because of the blindfold. They handed her back her backpack and within seconds she heard the car whirring up and by the time she had yanked the blindfold off her eyes, the car was already a speck in the distance.

She let out a long breath. She had done it!

12

Back in office, Fish-Eyes and Sona were closeted in his cabin. She ran the sound file of the interview on her phone and briefed him about the encounter. The wily Editor's eyes were gleaming. He was delighted that she had pulled it off so well. He wanted the interview in the next issue and he wanted it to be the coup of the year! She nodded, understanding his intentions perfectly.

She hugged the knowledge of the successful interview close to her, feeling that she would burst with the secret, longing to share it with Nafisa. Nafisa looked preoccupied nowadays, probably recovering from the super-successful International Conference in Casablanca. "She had a glow to her cheek lately and was smiling unnecessarily. It made her look even more beautiful," thought Sona.

She went and sat next to Ammi, who was shelling peas and watching TV. "Ammi", Sona said, "I've been able to find a small apartment on rent quite close to my office. It is not the same as living with you Ammi, but it will save me a lot of time and money as far as commuting is concerned. I have already paid the deposit. I can move into the apartment next week."

Ammi's hands stilled. She looked at Sona quietly and then said, "For me, you are like Nafisa. I do not know why I thought that you would be in this house forever. But beti, if you think that moving closer to your office is good for you, who am I to stop you?"

Sona moved closer to Ammi and took her hand in hers. "Ammi," she said, "I wish I could live here forever, but it is more practical to be closer to office. I can work longer and put in more hours. And Ammi, I'll be coming every Sunday to visit. I can't miss your lovely Sunday lunch."

The issue of *News* that Sona was waiting for with bated breath hit the stands the next week. Sona was flooded with phone calls. One of them was from Chibba, who declared himself entirely satisfied with the outcome!

Sona suppressed a smile. She had hardly planned to be the spokesperson for Chibba. But she had been careful to not let any value judgements leak into the article. She had allowed Chibba's voice to permeate the interview without letting her opinion getting superimposed on it. This was again something she had learnt from Shubhendu. As she re-read the article in the latest issue, she sneaked a look at Shubhendu Roy's cubicle. He was leaning back in his chair, with his hands on his chest and gazing at the ceiling. He assumed that pose when he was thinking deeply. He had been the first to congratulate her on the article, giving her an inscrutable look as he shook her hand.

The announcement that Sona was the winner of the prestigious Giridhar Dhir Award for the best investigative journalist of the year did not surprise her at all. At the office New Year party, Mr Jeevan Prabhu in a short speech congratulated Sona and chatted with her warmly for a long time. Sona spied Shubhendu Roy looking at her from a distance and felt an unnamed pang. She had not been able to talk to him freely somehow after the Chibba story. His presence irked her like a pebble inside the shoe.

After shifting to her new apartment, Sona kept up the tradition of spending Sundays at Ammi's place for a month. But slowly as work increased, the visits dwindled to two Sundays a month and now, three months down the line, Sona had not visited Ammi for an entire month. She had started getting work home and Sundays were equally if not more busy than working days. She made hurried weekly phone calls to Ammi and Nafisa and the phone calls to Mother and Rajeev became sporadic and hurried too. Often she was the first to come to office and the last to leave. She would see Shubhendu come at nine and leave at five. He came over once to her desk to ask her if she would come with him for a new play that had received rave reviews, but she refused because she was planning to finish her assignment over the weekend. It was not urgent, but she wanted to finish pending work, as she wanted to visit Shivagaon towards the end of the month. She wanted to be back at work during the visit of the British Prime Minister to India. She was hoping that Fish-Eyes would give her the assignment.

In his office, Mr Tiwari was looking thoughtfully at the schedule of the British Prime Minister. He wanted an interview and article on him. He called in

Shubhendu and the two men sat and looked at the schedule together. "I want you to go and meet him in Delhi, Shubhendu. You can take somebody else with you if you want," Tiwari said.

"I'd like to take Sona with me," Shubhendu said, "We are a good team."

The two men looked at each other for a long time. "She is using you, you know," Mr Tiwari said.

Shubhendu got up from his chair and said, "I'm allowing myself to be used. Don't we all use somebody?"

13

Sona was making this trip back to Shivagaon after a long time. Infact, after moving out of Ammi's place, this was her first visit. Rajeev had wanted her to come last month to organise a party at home for the Chairman of a German Company with whom *Geeta Engineering Works* had signed a big contract. But Sona had been unable to make it due to work commitments. Sona had stopped feeling guilty, after the initial months. The house was running smoothly enough.

She recalled her first visit to Shivagaon after her move to Mumbai. It was three weeks after her hasty departure. She and Rajeev were still smarting with unsaid accusing words. He had sent the driver to fetch her from the station. As the car entered the porch of the house and she got out, Dara bounded up to her, his tail wagging furiously and tongue hanging out. As she hugged him close, she was thankful that at least he held no grudges. "Wish we could be like dogs," she thought, "giving unconditional love."

She could see that in her absence, Ganpat had benevolently neglected the garden. The jasmine creeper pot near the entrance was nowhere to be seen and the guava tree by the compound wall had grown unruly. The lawn needed mowing and the hedge by the side badly required trimming. Ganpat was taking her little suitcase inside the house and giving a running commentary on the happenings of the past few weeks. Rajeev Saab had just returned from Germany and in his absence, the downstairs bathroom had choked up and flooded. He, Ganpat, had had to call the plumber who had demanded a neat amount to sort out the problem. The garden lights were getting fused too often and the electrician had taken a fat sum to set things right. Sona went in and looked at the house. The house seemed to put out its arms and embrace her. The house looked like a well-fed child who has everything except love and care. "Welcome home!" the house said, hugging her. She went up to her room to freshen up and after her cup of tea, the first thing she did was to take her cane basket out and gather the flowers and greens for the flower arrangements. She put the five glass vases of flowers in place and brought the house alive. Then, she turned to the kitchen and to Champabai, who was fussing around unnecessarily. Rajeev had promised to come home on time and Sona and Champabai planned a sumptuous dinner.

That first visit reminded Sona of all that she had left behind to build her life anew in Mumbai. Though Rajeev said that he understood her compulsions, she could not take his support for granted. As Sona became more and more involved in work, her visits to Shivagaon became less and less.

Sitting by the window seat now, Sona craned her neck. Nasrapur station was approaching. What was the little family up to? The charpoy was out in the sun and Savitri was sitting and chopping vegetables on it. Sonya was crawling on the ground. The girl could not be seen anywhere. But she was probably in school. Sona leaned back with a smile. The family was fine and all was well with the world. It would be well in Shivagaon too, she told herself, picking nervously at her cotton dupatta. Somewhere a niggling doubt had started gnawing at her brain. Rajeev had sounded cold, distant, and curt. Though Sona wanted to attribute it to his busy life and hectic workload, it was disturbing her peace of mind.

Back in her house, she immediately allowed herself to be sucked into her old routine. She had chalked out that routine for herself when she had entered this house as a new bride. After her shower, as she relaxed with a mug of coffee that Champabai got for her, she called up Pushpa for a long chat. Pushpa was her best friend in Shivagaon, her only friend. She was a post-graduate in English Literature from Madras University. She had had a job as a lecturer in a Chennai college, when she had met and fallen in love with Arvind. He was an IIT graduate, who had started this factory in Shivagaon. Pushpa and given up her life in Chennai, her job, her Carnatic music classes, her family, and followed her husband to another State, to a little village infact, where she hardly had any intellectual stimulation. But she had settled into her life in a tranquil fashion. Arvind, who was a Maharashtrian, was very protective about his lovely Tamilian Brahmin wife. They sent their two children to boarding school when they completed their sixth standard. Arvind and Pushpa were deliriously in love with each other even so many years after their marriage. Pushpa had a beautiful garden, a wonderful personal library, and a close set of friends with whom she socialised on a regular basis. She also wrote. She was the author of two volumes of poetry. They did not earn her much money but got her enough literary acclaim to be invited for the annual seminars of various literary bodies, including the Sahitya Akademi. She was a fairly good painter and had had an exhibition at one of the famous galleries of Mumbai. She did not sell many canvases but she got excellent reviews, which were enough for her to be invited for artistic gatherings held at Kala Ghoda. Pushpa was in her thirties, but she looked much younger. She was a fitness freak and took time out every day for yoga, pranayama and meditation. Her skin glowed. Her long hair had not a single grey and her supple body had all the right curves in the right places. Pushpa looked like a woman who was loved by life and who loved life back.

Sona and Pushpa had had many conversations after Sona's shift to Mumbai. The residual guilty conscience within Sona made her question her move away from Shivagaon and she sought a validation from somebody whose opinion she valued. "How can you allow your talents to wither away in a backwater like Shivagaon, Pushpa?" Sona had asked, "You would have gone places if you had stuck on in a big city like Chennai. Your painting, your music, your literature…what possible scope is there for you in Shivagaon? What is there for you here?"

"Arvind!" Pushpa had said. "Arvind is here. And he is what matters the most."

"But what about your individuality... What are you getting here?"

"Happiness!" Pushpa said, "I have no desire to move anywhere else. I want to be by Arvind's side. Anything in life will be meaningless if I don't wake up in the morning with Arvind by my side!"

Sona could say nothing to counter that!

After the usual pleasantries, Pushpa asked her how long she intended to stay.

"Three days", Sona said jokingly, "I think I'm needed more in my office than here."

But Pushpa did not laugh. "Don't make yourself so dispensable Sona", she said.

"What do you mean?" Sona said.

Then Pushpa described the party that Rajeev had organised for the Chairman of the German Company. Preeti was the official hostess for the occasion and Pushpa told in detail how dependent Rajeev seemed on Preeti. She described how confidently Preeti moved about the house, managing snacks, ensuring that the served food was hot, and looking after the entertainment and comfort of guests, most importantly, ensuring that Rajeev was comfortable. Throughout the evening, the two of them moved in tandem, signalling to each other across the room.

Sona listened in silence, picturing the party in her mind, unsurprised now why Rajeev had not elaborated on the party, when Sona had asked him later how it had gone. The unease in her mind grew and by the time Rajeev came home that evening, Sona was ready with a list of cutting questions to which she received a list of sarcastic answers. They slept in separate rooms that night and Sona announced to Rajeev her intention of returning to Mumbai the next day.

"Fine", Rajeev said, "The driver will drop you at the station. I have to leave early for office tomorrow to prepare for the video-conference with my Japanese clients."

Back in the train, Sona sat subdued and quiet as the barren landscape hurtled past the window. The train slowed down at Nasrapur and Sona saw the stationmaster hurrying towards the train engine. She looked out eagerly for a glimpse of the little family, but all was silent today. Sona sat back with a sigh. "They were gone for a little outing," she told herself. They would surely be back.

Then another thought struck her. Savitri had had enough of her boring husband and tedious life in this back-of-beyond place. She had taken her children and gone off to her own village... Never to come back perhaps. But what life would she have there? She would just be a meddlesome addition to her maternal home, an irritant to her new sister-in-law who ruled the kitchen now. All her friends were married now. They have settled into domesticity with husbands no better or even worse than hers. The river was her only friend. And by the banks of this river she spent her lonely evenings. Sona slapped herself mentally. Sometimes she let her fertile imagination too loose.

Savitri was just out shopping for vegetables for the evening dinner. Her boring but nevertheless, dutiful husband would soon be back, hungry and tired. Savitri would serve him hot rotis and his favourite vegetable. He would comment on the blandness of the vegetable and she would promise to prepare tambda rassa on Sunday. Hot, spicy, rich, just the way her husband liked it. Sona felt a great sob rise inside her. "Poor, poor Savitri!" She thought, "You are caught now, aren't you?"

Back in Mumbai, she called up Fish-Eyes to let him know that she was back earlier than promised. "Oh good Sona!" He said, "I had a dinner date with Mr Peter Griffith of *The World Today* magazine tonight, but I'm feeling unwell. I have already booked a table for two at The Chimney Restaurant at Radisson Orbit. I do not want to cancel. Please fill in for me. I know it is short notice, but Peter Griffith has been a good friend to *News* and with the impending visit of the British PM, his cooperation will be even more welcome. Go and enjoy yourself. Charm him. The Chimney makes excellent soufflé, I've heard."

"Just three hours to prepare for dinner... Wonder whether my favourite sari is ironed... I need to paint my nails and shampoo my hair. What kind of a man is this Mr Griffith?" Thoughts ran amok in Sona's mind as she quickly got herself mentally ready for the outing-cum-assignment.

As she hurriedly ironed the blouse that was to go with the sari, she thought of the likely topics of conversation. Rajeev, Preeti, and the successful party that they had organised together, were already forgotten.

Mr Griffith turned out to be an excellent dinner companion. He was silver-haired, with an aristocratic and angular face. He was a fountain of knowledge on Western music, philosophy and cinema. Sona just sat and listened. She was utterly charmed. She forgot to smile and bat her eyelashes. There was nothing fake or put-on about him. This man was hundred percent genuine.

Two hours passed as though on silver wings. When they were done with the soufflé and were having coffee, she saw a handsome young guy, bearded and tall, pass them two tables away. And clinging to his arm and laughing and looking radiant and beautiful was the white sari-clad figure of Nafisa!

The two were so absorbed in each other that they passed out of the door without paying any attention to the people around. Sona kept down her coffee cup, her mouth agape. Mr Griffith's deep voice receded in the background and her mind leapt to all kinds of impossible conjectures. Sona was surprised at the surge of jealousy that coursed through her heart. Nafisa could not have an admirer. She was the most virginal of women alive. She was the epitome of purity and innocence. Men, lust, and sex were alien words when connected with Nafisa. She could not, simply could not have a man in her life!

14

Nafisa woke up with the ping on her mobile. She picked it up, smiled as she read the message, and started typing a reply. It was Sunday today and she could afford to laze in bed. She was deeply, deeply happy with the languorous turn her days had taken lately.

When she got up, she rooted around in her notes and books lying on her crowded table and fished out a ragged notepad. She turned to a page on which she had scribbled a poem two or three years ago while she sat in the back seats of yet another University seminar and listened to an old man drone on about geopolitical strategies adopted by USA towards the Indian subcontinent. She had been feeling very vulnerable that day. She had looked into the mirror in the morning that day and spotted the first grey hair on her head and had suddenly become afraid, afraid of time passing her by, afraid of aging and afraid of death.

Standing barefoot in her billowing nightdress, Nafisa re-read the poem that made her feel immensely lonely each time she went through it.

Musings

I grow old, I grow old.
Thirty summers have quietly rolled.
And I, only half-awake
Sleep-walked through the give-and-take
Of the business, that is life.

My talks are hailed, my books are read.
I'm able to earn more than my bread.
I sing, paint, read, and write.
No husband or children shatter the quiet
Of my zealous, creative evenings.

I spied today my first grey hair.
And I haven't had time to stand and stare
For life was a hectic merry-go-round
Of meetings, classes, lectures, tours.

A white cat shares my board and bed.
As chaste as I am and well-bred.
But both of us now are growing old.
I hold her closer to keep out the cold.
But why have my specs gone foggy and my
cheeks wet?

I wrap a shawl over my thin chest.
Whatever happens, happens for the best.
Sometimes the evenings are lonely.
But students and colleagues see only
A thirty-year old smiling public woman.

Nafisa sighed as she kept the notebook back.
She peeped at her reflection in the oval mirror in her
room. Were the dark circles under her eyes getting
darker? She rubbed the frown line between her eyes.
It made her look aged. Then she widened her eyes
and slapped herself on the cheek. "Nafisa! Dr Nafisa
Ahmed! Stop behaving like a shallow doll!"

It was a Sunday and Sona called up Ammi and
told her that she would be visiting. Ammi was in the

kitchen when Sona reached the house. She went and greeted Ammi and then asked where Nafisa was. "In her room," Ammi said, "Probably on the phone with Khaled."

Sona looked at Ammi with round eyes, "You know?"

"Of course! Nafisa never hides anything from me. He was here for two days. He left on Friday. He is a nice man, and she is a big girl. Surely she is old enough to decide what's good for her and what's not."

Sona shook her head in disbelief. "I'm going up," she said.

Nafisa was not on the phone. She was typing on her laptop. She looked as ethereal as ever. Impossible to think of her with that lover-boy!

Nafisa faced Sona's barrage of questions with the calm composure that was her hallmark. "We are best friends. You are supposed to tell me things, especially something as important as a new boyfriend." Sona was sounding high-pitched because of emotion.

Nafisa and Khaled had met in Casablanca, during that International Conference that turned out to be a success in many ways. After the first session, on the first day, when Nafisa returned to her seat, she found a single long-stemmed rose on her seat. A little note stuck to the stem said, "Your silent admirer!" It was so high school tacky that Nafisa started looking around for a school boy in the assembled crowd. Of course, she could not spot her admirer. But she carried the rose with her all through the day and took it back with her to the hotel where she was staying. The next day, as she came back to her seat after the first session, there was a long-stemmed red rose on the chair again! The note said, "To the most beautiful woman in the room!" No school boy in sight today as well. On the third and final day of the Conference, when she came back to her seat, there was no red rose. But as she took her seat, with a twinge of disappointment in her heart, the young and handsome bearded guy sitting to her right, held a red rose in front of her.

"Hello", he smiled, "I'm Khaled."

He was a doctoral student at the University and had been following her closely since the first day. Nafisa noticed that he had sparkling white teeth and a low-pitched voice that went very well with his quaintly accented English. Nafisa did not attend the rest of the sessions, but strolled along with Khaled to the campus café, listening to him talk and allowing herself to be charmed.

"You do know that I'm seven years older than you," she said.

"Yes, Dr Nafisa Ahmed", he smiled, "But I'm not proposing marriage to you here!"

She was delighted with his boyish repartees. Here was a guy, who was not overwhelmed by her academic persona. He was intelligent and observant and he was smitten with her. Nafisa was not a shallow woman but as she grew older and her days became more and more crowded with Senate meetings, writing papers, preparing for her lectures, and taking notes for her books, she felt that there was something missing in her life…that she was leading a life that was totally in her head. She felt that the emotional part of her had been overwhelmed or suppressed, and that she had been denied even a sight of The Lake of Pleasure that others enjoyed so easily. She mostly moved amongst people older than she was. She was getting afraid that she had picked up many of their fuddy-duddy mannerisms. She had resigned herself to believe that love and pleasure and erotic joy was not hers to have. Though she, in her serene and composed outward appearance, seemed to be above all these temporal delights, in her heart, she was sad that she had been decreed only half a life by Fate.

Then Khaled came. He released the many Nafisas chained invisibly. One by one, the many Nafisas floated out on butterfly wings. With his corny jokes and his romantic gestures, he brought into her life a balance between the intellectual and emotional lives that she had been longing for until now.

"And what is the future of this relationship?" Sona asked.

"I don't know," Nafisa said, "He's coming to Mumbai for two years now as part of a project his University is working on and will be staying in the room you vacated. After two years, who knows?"

Sona could not believe her ears, "Ammi is okay with this arrangement?"

"Of course. I consulted her before proposing all this to Khaled. I got the project he is working on passed by our University in the last Senate meeting. So all he has to do now is book a ticket and climb into a plane."

The two women looked at each other in silence. "He's using you, you know," Sona said.

Nafisa shrugged, "We all use somebody!"

There was a ping on her mobile and Nafisa bit her smile back as she picked it up. "Excuse me Sona," Nafisa said, "This is urgent!"

15

"I can't believe that Nafisa is behaving in this giddy fashion! She used to be so balanced, so stable, and now she goes around with that love-struck expression on her face and a foolish smile on her lips and a glazed look in her eyes. It is nauseating!" Sona said to Shubhendu when they were having dinner at a nice little restaurant in Delhi. The interview with the British PM had gone off very well in the morning. Shubhendu Roy was taking the midnight flight back to Mumbai and Sona was going back to stay with her mother. She was spending a day with her before returning to Mumbai. But now, sitting with Shubhendu and sharing a meal and titbits about her life with him seemed almost like old times. The initial awkwardness she had felt with him had been dispelled by his easy and carefree mannerism.

She bit into her excellent naan and chewed it appreciatively. "Nafisa is behaving totally out of character," she said.

Shubhendu looked at her and laughed, "So the Idyllic Female Paradise has finally been violated! And not by me!"

Sona gave a wry laugh.

"But tell me, why are we talking of Nafisa and her young boyfriend? Don't we have anything else to talk about?"

"Like what?"

"Like why you are sitting with me and having dinner and not sitting with your mother?"

Sona looked down at her plate of food. Mother had asked her to come home for dinner. Sona had avoided it. She did not want another interrogative session where she would spend her time defending each and every decision she made in her life. Sona called her back and promised to be with her as soon as she finished dinner. This dinner with Shubhendu was something that needed to be done. She wanted to look him in the eye again and acknowledge wordlessly and silently his role in her success. She was immensely relieved when he accepted her invitation without any rancour or outward sign of sulkiness. It was such a comfort to sit with him, to listen to his quiet and calm voice and discuss with him all the latest songs, books and films.

When as usual he asked her, "What's up with your life partner?" She told him everything uncensored. "Let's be fair to Nafisa Aunty!" Shubhendu laughed, "She deserves romance in her life like anybody else!"

"Love! Romance!" Sona said, "Trivial pursuits! They are meant for the ordinary! Dr Nafisa Ahmad is marked out for something much higher than these ordinary preoccupations of average people."

Sona came to '7, Jaisingh Marg' late at night. The appointment bungalow of the Minister for Civil Aviation lay at the end of a heavily guarded lane. The bungalows of ministers and judges of the Supreme

Court flanked the quiet lane. Sona paid the taxi, showed her identity to the sentry at the gate and went in. Mother was in her study, sifting through files. Sona was struck anew by how elegant Mother looked even in her slightly crumpled cotton saree and slightly dishevelled short hair. She became acutely conscious of her faded jeans and the crumpled white shirt that she had been wearing since morning. She cleared her throat, "Mother," she said from the doorway, "I'm home!"

Mother looked up from her files and turned to her. Sona pulled her favourite flame-orange sleeveless jacket straight and smiled. "Sona!" Mrs Kamla Pradhan got up from her chair and took off her glasses, "Go and change dear! I'll just finish this last file and then we can have hot chocolate in the hall outside."

"Yes Mother", Sona said from the doorway and fled.

As it turned out, the late night hot chocolate session did not turn out to be such an ordeal after all. Mother asked her questions about her life but did not question the answers she gave. She just listened in silence. Sona felt more confident about facing Mother after winning the Giridhar Dhir award. It had seemed to Sona earlier that her decision to leave Shivagaon had caused more turmoil in Mother's mind than it had in her own. Though it was Mother, who had discouraged Sona from getting into matrimony so early and hastily, it had seemed to Sona that Mother treated Rajeev with more courtesy, consideration and care than even Sona. Her mother's behaviour towards Rajeev had changed tremendously after the incident of their first and memorable wedding anniversary. Whenever Sona talked about her personal life, Mother's immediate response was, "And what does Rajeev think?"

It had irritated Sona at that time, but she slowly realised that Mother wanted her to work harder on her marriage. Mother always wanted Sona to work harder on everything she did. What she actually did was never enough! It seemed hypocritical to Sona that Mother should prioritise Rajeev's opinion over hers, considering that she herself had never deferred to her husband's wishes.

The memory of a long-ago afternoon stung her again. She was sitting on the carpet playing with a doll. Sumati Aji was talking to her mother, who was slicing apples.

"Kamle", she said in her loud and grating voice, "What are you going to do with this girl of yours? She is so dark and slight. She is exactly her father's copy. Why didn't she inherit your looks?"

"Looks, brains, character... They are all fated", Mother said, as she passed her Aunt a plate of apple slices, "It is all a matter of chance."

"Still", Sumati Aji said, biting into a slice and continuing to talk about Sona as though she were a retarded child, unable to understand what was being said about her, "Still, I feel worried. She is so small. Look at her! She is nearly ten and does not even look eight! What will she grow up to be? Who will marry her?"

"Let us cross the fences when we come to them. Why peer so far into the future? Anyway, it is too early to think about marriage and all that for her. My Sona is going to be a doctor, a skilled and famed gynaecologist. When you have talent and success, people forget to talk about your looks."

"But", Sumati Aji persisted munching furiously, "Looks are important for a girl and like it or not, marriage is important too."

"Oh, let's change the topic," Mother said, wiping her hands on a paper napkin, "All girls get married, even plain-looking girls. That is no big deal. See, even you got married. Isn't that a wonder Atya? Someone married you too." Mother laughed loudly, a forceful laugh that signalled the end of the discussion. A small figure got up from the carpet and scampered inside with a doll clutched to the heart.

To this day, Sona had not forgotten Sumati Aji's words. And each time she recalled them, they wounded her with fresh intensity.

Sona put down the book she was reading and stared blankly at the wall opposite. What was it that her mother had said? Something about success... Only success, she had said, could make you invulnerable in this world.

The Giridhar Dhir award somehow justified the move back to Mumbai. Sona talked to Mother about work and the move to her new apartment and the morning interview with the British PM and her plans to write a book. Mother just listened quietly and to Sona's immense relief, but also puzzlement, did not ask a single question to her answers.

16

Sona's second wedding anniversary passed quietly enough, so quietly infact that she almost missed the date on the calendar. She and Shubhendu were working hard on a new assignment that entailed frequent trips to the interiors of Maharashtra. Rajeev was out of the country on a work trip. He called from Germany and they spoke politely, until the conversation petered out and they had nothing to say to each other. Sona kept the phone down and was surprised to find that she did not feel any emotion. No regret, no anger, no sorrow... Nothing. She recalled her first wedding anniversary and felt great sympathy for the Sona she had been then. That Sona was vulnerable, needy, sensitive, and touchy. How she had longed and longed for Rajeev that day! And he was not there! Her heart broke that day. When Rajeev explained to her all that had happened at the factory that night, she had nodded, not with understanding, but with resignation. "That factory Rajeev!" she said to him, "It will always lie between us."

"Is it my fault that the fire should happen on this particular night?" Rajeev asked hotly.

"No. But it is as though the factory made sure that you would not be with me on our special night."

"You talk about the factory as though it is a woman!"

"Worse than that!" Sona said, "I can't discuss the situation with the factory as I could have with a woman!"

Sona's trips to Shivagaon dwindled as days passed. Rajeev and she spoke to each other at least once in a day, but the conversation lasted for hardly six or seven minutes. It was a duty they performed. It was ironical that Sona understood the fire that drove Rajeev to succeed when she no longer cared. Her own fire, her own flight to success, her own ambition took precedence now.

And truly, Sona was on fire now-a-days. She was putting in extra hours at work, reading in the library for the book she was planning. She was writing a thriller novel, which required a bit of research. It was as though she was immersing herself in work to stop herself from thinking. Her Sunday visits to Ammi's place had almost come to a stop. With Khaled there, the Idyllic Female Paradise no longer existed. It was no longer a sanctuary, which she had thought it to be. She spoke to Nafisa and Ammi occasionally on the phone, but rarely met up. Khaled's presence in Nafisa's life bothered her more than she could acknowledge to herself. She tried to speak of this to Mother and expected some support from there, but most surprisingly, Mother said not a word against Nafisa. Mother rarely called her nowadays. Though this was what Sona had always wanted, once Mother actually stopped calling three times in a day, Sona felt let down.

Sona's Sundays were spent with Shubhendu. Either he came over to her place or she went to his house. They cooked together and then put on a film to watch after lunch. Sometimes they just sat in the same room and read their individual books like an old married couple. Sometimes they listened to music, together, not on their individual i-pods. They were very comfortable with each other and if a Sunday passed when Sona could not be with Shubhendu, she missed him. He was her bestfriend in the world, but he was not her lover. This was something that was new for Sona. She had always believed that Platonic friendships between men and women were a myth. It was true that there was a frisson of attraction between herself and Shubhendu but it was more from his side than her side. She had drawn an invisible line around herself and Shubhendu respected it. Sona, for a strange reason, never raised the temperature between them. She cherished the friendship between them more than any likely romantic involvement and was keen to keep their friendship uncomplicated with passion.

Days were flying. It was in the midst of one such day that Sona got a call from Shivagaon. It was Champabai. She was sounding hysterical. Rajeev Saheb was running a high temperature. He had not been well for two days but kept going to office for some urgent work. But this morning, when he did not come out of the room, Champabai went and found him delirious with fever. Ganpat got the doctor home to examine him and the doctor gave an injection and some medicine. He said that there was nothing serious as of now, but it was very important to keep the temperature down. Champabai and Ganpat had been taking turns to apply cold strips of cloth on his forehead but Champabai insisted that only Sona could now handle the situation. "You have to come Vahini sahib… Come quickly! Sahib needs you…needs you now…or…or…it will be too late…" Champabai trailed off with a sob.

"Champabai, control yourself. He will be fine. Sahib will be fine. Give him plenty of water to drink, give the medicines on time, and keep applying the cold strips… Hold the fort until I come. I am taking the evening train and coming. Still it will be eight in the night by the time I reach… Handle the situation till then. Do not worry Champabai, nothing will happen to your sahib. Thank you for telling me."

Sona kept down the phone with less confidence than she had shown in her voice. A feeling of panic gripped her, a vague guilt for being far when her husband needed her near him. She quickly booked a taxi for the station and went to Fish-Eyes' office to inform him and ask for leave for a couple of days. Then she went home and packed hurriedly. By the time, her little suitcase was ready, the taxi had come and she locked up the flat and was on her way to the railway station.

She called up Champabai to tell her that she was on her way. Sahib's temperature was not coming down, Champabai said and the panic in her voice turned Sona's heart cold. As the train approached Nasrapur station, Sona craned her neck. Darkness enveloped the little house where the stationmaster's family lived. The light filtering out through the window gave proof of their existence inside. Savitri, Saguna and Sonya were inside, doing what they usually did at this hour. Savitri was cooking, Saguna was doing her homework and Sonya was playing with his train engine. The stationmaster was probably hurrying towards the engine driver's cabin. All was well with the little family. Sona's overheated brain felt a little relief. She leaned back and closed her eyes, the little lighted window cooling her emotions like a whiff of cold air.

Sona rushed to Rajeev's bedside the moment she reached the house. He was sleeping, but his face looked drawn with illness. It was a strange kind of viral fever which had attacked him. It even flummoxed the doctor. Sona placed her cool palm on Rajeev's forehead, "I'm here Raj", she murmured, "close to you."

His eyes fluttered open. He put his hand on hers and closed his eyes again. Then he turned on his side and was soon fast asleep. Champabai, who had almost fallen into Sona's arms with relief, ran downstairs in the kitchen to prepare the herbal concoction that Sona told her to make. Sona quietly got up and went into the bathroom to change and freshen up. It was around midnight when Rajeev got up. Sona was dozing by his side. But she awoke the moment he stirred. She went down and got him the hot khichdi that she had prepared for him. They did not talk much, but Sona could see the relief on his face as he ate his light meal. He said that his head ached, and she slid his head onto her lap and massaged his head lightly, her touch giving him more comfort than any medicine in the world possibly could. After a while, he clasped her hand in his and just lay still. "Thank you for coming Sona," he said. "Shhhhh...sleep now! How did you even think that I would not come when you called", Sona said. She patted him on his head and he slept. Rajeev slipped in and out of delirious fever for four days. Sona spent all her time by his side. She called up Fish-Eyes and extended her leave. She informed Mother, Ammi, Nafisa and Shubhendu about the developments. She put the house and garden in order whenever she could find the time.

Seven days passed. It was clear that Rajeev had surmounted whatever virus had attacked him. He was round the bend. It was rest and care that he needed more than medicines or intrusive treatment. Exactly seven days after Sona had come to Shivagaon, Rajeev sat up in bed, looking much fresher than before. "Not khichdi again", he complained, "Give me something more solid today."

"Okay my dear patient", Sona smiled, "It seems that you are ready to join the world of the living again!"

That evening Sona returned to Mumbai. Rajeev came down to the porch to bid her farewell. Sona put her hand to his cheek. "Take care Rajeev", she said. "Call me whenever you need me. Do not hesitate. I am there for you. As I know, you are there for me!" And she was gone.

As Rajeev turned to go inside, his heart filled with desolation so extreme that he had to close his eyes and shake his head to recover his equilibrium. Sona had warned him to stay away from office for two more days. He was to stay at home, watch TV if he so desired, read light books, relax, chat with friends over the phone and strictly avoid shoptalk.

As Champabai fussed about in the kitchen, Rajeev fiddled in the hall cabinet where Sona had kept the photo albums, neatly stacked and labelled. As he pulled out the album labelled "Pre-wedding", he realised that this was probably the first time that he had taken the time to take a look at the photos that Sona had so meticulously filed and captioned.

Dara came and sat by his feet and Rajeev allowed him to peep into the albums that he scanned. There was a snap of Sona's where she was dressed in an elaborate ghaghra-choli and lots of silver jewellery. Rajeev remembered this dress distinctly. Sona had worn it on the day she had proposed to him. They had gone for dinner at a newly opened eating joint, quite posh and up-market. He had clicked the picture and only then asked her why she was not smiling. To his utter distress, Sona had started crying. She said that she had had a big showdown with her mother before coming out to meet him. Mother had returned home earlier than anticipated, and had immediately asked Sona where she was going in 'that fancy dress'. When Sona had replied that she was meeting Rajeev, her mother had sat her down and given her an hour-long lecture on self-respect, duty, ambition and success. She had warned Sona that getting into a relationship at this stage was a sure recipe of destroying her blossoming career. Sona had argued and the argument had flared into a fight and the fight had grown into a major showdown. So much so that Sona said that she would not return home that night and would spend the night in Rajeev's apartment. Rajeev had shuddered to imagine what Sona's mother's reaction would be to that! He had somehow pacified Sona who could hardly eat a morsel and they had quickly paid the bill and gone for a walk on the beach. There, holding his hand in a tight grip Sona had asked in a small voice, "Rajeev, will you marry me?"

"Of course Sona", he had said, "I am serious about you. Of course I'll marry you!"

"Now?"

He had faltered. *Geeta Engineering Works* was still not on its feet and he wanted to give the factory his full attention before getting into matrimony.

"Soon?" And her voice was urgent.

"Rajeev," she said, "If the answer is not yes, then we will have to part ways."

He had taken her in his arms and said yes. He could not let her go.

Within a month, they were married and Sona Pradhan became Mrs Sona Jaykar.

In the album labelled 'Wedding', Sona was looking radiant, all her dusky beauty shining through. Mrs Kamala Pradhan looked austere and grave. His mother-in-law's attitude towards him softened as days went by. She even deigned to hold a conversation with him if he picked up the landline phone at home when she called her daughter. He could understand why Sona felt so oppressed by her mother. Sona was right. Her mother was a cold and distant woman, incapable of understanding love or lovers.

As Rajeev scanned the album labelled 'Shivagaon', he came upon pictures mostly of him and his factory. There were plenty of pictures of factory functions where Sona had been invited. This was the picture clicked during the Diwali party held for factory colleagues. It was a group photo. Next to Rajeev, dressed in a sequined pink sari, Preeti stood smiling, her long thick hair tied in a serpentine plait. Rajeev smiled involuntarily as he fingered her picture. It was so rare to find women with such long and lustrous hair nowadays. His mother used to keep her hair in a long plait and long hair reminded him strongly of his mother. She cut it into a short bob after she went to the US. But he always gave a second look to women with long hair. It was one symbol of femininity, which made him deeply nostalgic. That and women who wore saris. Young women rarely draped saris nowadays. By giving up long hair and saris, they had freed themselves from cumbersome ideas of beauty and he partly agreed with the logic, yet, his head always turned when he caught sight of a young woman with long hair or who carried off a sari with grace. Preeti wore sarees every day, allowing her long, thick plait to snake down to below her waist. He would never admit it openly to anyone, but one of the prime reasons why he chose her over the other candidates was because of her long, thick hair and the fact that she wore her sari so elegantly. That she was eminently suitable to be his PA became clear soon enough. She had a sweet, accommodating nature. She was trustworthy. She never gossiped or talked loosely with anyone. She hero-worshipped him and though it was not in her job profile, took it upon herself to bring him his coffee, tea, lime juice just when he wanted it most. He needed her more than he cared to admit, yet she made it seem that she needed him, or rather the job he gave her, more. She came from a very humble background. She was a fatherless girl. It was only because her mother was a clerk in a convent school that she had been able to get an English-medium education. She had done well in studies, acquired a B.Com degree and finished a secretarial course while working on the side. This job meant a lot to her. Her mother had retired the previous year. Her younger brother had just finished his B.Com and on the recommendation of Rajeev immediately had a job at a nearby factory belonging to Rajeev's IIT batch mate.

How happy Preeti had been on the day her brother got the job! She had visited him at his home that Sunday with a box of sweets. Rajeev had finished his solitary Sunday brunch and was browsing the Sunday papers. Champabai and Ganpat generally had the day off after eleven every Sunday and they were out. Preeti put a piece of pedha in his mouth and bent down to touch his feet. This old-fashioned gesture moved him. He hurriedly raised her up by her shoulders and he saw that tears filled her eyes. He cupped her sweet, plump face in his hands. He looked at her kohl-rimmed eyes, the bindi on her forehead, and the loose tendrils of hair around her head… He brought her face close and their breaths mingled. Suddenly, as though coming to his senses, he removed his hands with a jerk. The confusion in her eyes made him kick himself mentally and he hurriedly took a step back. "I…I'm sorry!" he mumbled, "I can't do this…you are too beautiful and too good for this… you deserve something better…I don't know what came over me."

He did not know then, why Preeti gave a huge sob and picking up her bag ran out of the house. She did not turn up in office for the next two days, pleading sick leave. When she came, she was subdued, quieter than before, avoiding eye contact with him and going about her work as though a vital spark had gone out of her.

It took days for her to come back to normal and he could breathe freely again, when she gave him once more that sweet dimpled smile when he entered his cabin and wished him good morning. She had almost become his alter ego, and he did not know when he had started discussing the stresses of his job with her. The Chinese clients were difficult, the meeting with the minister simply had to go smoothly, the Floor Supervisor needed to be pulled up for showing favouritism, the female staff felt unsafe with the new canteen manager…these and many issues that Rajeev wanted to air to someone, he aired to Preeti. The best thing about her was that she listened silently, giving her opinion only when asked. Yet, she was super-efficient. The way she had organised the party at his home when the German clients had come, made his regard for her rise several notches higher. When he had fallen sick now and the doctor advised complete rest, he had asked Champabai to call up Preeti, fully confident that she would drop everything and be by his bedside. But Champabai had gone and called up Sona. And Sona came.

Rajeev did not tell Champabai to call Sona because he would not have been able to bear another refusal from her. Preeti he knew would come. She was his subordinate. She needed him or at least, she needed the job he gave her. Preeti made him feel needed, as the new Sona did not. Now he needed Sona. It hurt Rajeev's manly pride to feel needy. Yet, when Sona came, he healed. Healed faster than he cared to admit.

17

Kamla Pradhan finished the last file and removed her reading glasses. It had been a long day and now, it was past ten. She felt tired today. As she put off the lights of the study and headed for her bedroom, she wondered about old age. She never thought of herself as old. She was very particular with her workout regimen, alternating yoga, gym, swimming and long walks through the week. She watched her diet and was careful with the kind of saris she wore. She had had the same hairstyle for years. But through several trials and errors this was what suited her best. Kamla Pradhan was not a vain woman. She put core values like duty, service and dedication above physical beauty. For this reason, she hardly wore any jewellery or make-up. Her saris were always simple cotton. She had wanted her daughter to be like her as well---simple and strong and valuing inner beauty more than outer.

When she was pregnant, she had prayed for a dark complexioned daughter, simply because, such a girl, born with this handicap in India, would work doubly hard on her other strengths. She got her wish. She got a dark-complexioned daughter. She named her Sona... Sona for gold... She wanted her daughter to turn everything she touched to gold. But what was Sona doing? Did she even know what she was doing?

No doubt, she had won the Giridhar Dhir Award. But what was going on with her marriage? Who was this Shubhendu guy? Why was Rajeev okay with all this? Did Sona want this marriage or not? The marriage, which she had entered into so hastily, defying her mother and sacrificing her career. But the moment she got what she wanted, she lost interest in it. She wanted to be in some other place, always in some other place. Just like her father!

Kamla Pradhan sat in front of her dressing table and brushed her short curly hair vigorously. Then she brushed her teeth and washed her face. As she creamed her face with the night cream that she had recently picked up at Heathrow airport, she looked critically at her face. It was a face which she liked. But it had deep lines around the mouth and between the eyebrows. There were dark circles under the eyes but Kamla Pradhan valued each line and blemish. She would never have consented to have these lines erased. They were signifiers of a life lived, of time endured, and of battles fought. They added to her stature as a wise woman of the world. Except that she did not feel like a wise woman and even less like a wise old woman. There had been choices she had made. Those hard choices had bequeathed her a lifetime of solitariness. But they were *her* choices and therefore never to be regretted. Kamla rubbed the night cream on her face thoughtfully. It was a solitary existence, but not lonely. Her work made a tremendous difference to lives... Many lives. That was compensation enough for a single existence. It was, was it not?

Just then, her mobile rang. She was rattled. Who was calling at this hour? Was Sona okay? She rushed to pick up her mobile. "Vikrant!" "Vikrant!" The screen flashed.

"Vikrant?" she breathed.

"Darling!" he said, "My love!"

Her heart heaved, as she said, "Is everything okay? Why are you calling me so late? Where is Swaroop?"

"She's asleep in the bedroom. I'm out in the hall. I can't sleep tonight." There was a pause. "I miss you!"

Kamla clutched her bedpost. "Don't play this game with me Vikrant!" she said, "You worry about your sensitive wife. That is your duty is not it? Leave me to do my duty."

"Is that all you have to say to me?" Vikrant's voice was strained.

Kamla's heart was thumping loudly. "Vikrant!" she sobbed, "My darling! My Love!"

18

Sona was sitting in Ammi's living room, knitting. She had picked up this new hobby following the advice of Ammi. She had confessed to Ammi a few weeks ago that she had difficulty going to sleep as her head buzzed too much. It was as though there was a lot of traffic in her brain. Ammi advised her to bring a couple of balls of bright coloured wool, a pair of knitting needles and knit a scarf for her. "Knit for half an hour at least before going to sleep. Your mind will relax and at the end of a few days, you will have a beautiful hand-knitted scarf to show for your efforts. Meditation-cum-constructive activity," the ever-practical Ammi said. Though she had laughed at Ammi then, she had nevertheless gone and bought the wool. Now, as she knitted silently and steadily, she understood the wisdom of Ammi's advice. With every click of the needle, with every knit and purl, her tightly wound brain slowly unspooled. As the length of the scarf increased, the stormy ripples in her head eased. She submitted herself quietly to the giving and taking of woollen stitches on the knitting needles. In fact, this was the first piece of knitting that she was doing since she came to Mumbai six months ago. Life had become so frenetic that she had been swept off her feet in the on - rushing tide. But as she tidily clicked on the needles, she realised that she actually quite enjoyed spending her evenings doing some crochet or tatting or knitting or painting. She had always had artistic and creative leanings and this kind of work relaxed her mentally. As her fingers mechanically danced an intricate and delicate dance with the needles, her mind wound tightly with the tensions of the day, slowly began to unfurl. Thoughts, images, sounds of today, last week, last decade began to float loosely like astronauts in zero - gravity.

A memory landed softly and other images began to coalesce around it. Rajeev was lying in bed, with his eyes closed and face gaunt. Worry and terror fringed the seven days that she had spent nursing him. At one time, his temperature had shot up so high that she had been afraid he would slip into a coma. Frantically laying cold strips of cloth on his forehead and sponging him with a cold and damp cloth she had prayed as she'd never prayed before. But he'd recovered just as quickly as he'd fallen ill. Dr Gokhale attributed his fast recovery to his young and healthy body unsullied by drugs, alcohol or tobacco. The medicine given to him had therefore worked like magic. Her seven days of leave were over and she returned to *News*. Rajeev was well again and needed her no longer. She had been to Shivagaon twice after his illness and was glad to see him healthy and fighting fit again. The morning jogs with Dara had started again and so had the work-outs. Dr Gokhale had told him to take it easy on the work and she had made Rajeev promise that he would return home by five every evening and not bring work home.

A new tenderness had sprung up between them now, though he had not yet said anything about her job and her living away from him.

"Peace of mind was the first casualty of this fast-paced digital world," she thought. When people had little cottage industries inside their homes, it kept them gainfully employed throughout the day. They worked with their hands, seeing the end-product with their own eyes at the conclusion of their labour. The Industrial Revolution took away this uniqueness of production from humans and bestowed a factory-full of perfect, machine-made products to the market. The digital age speeded up this process and shortened people's memory and attention span. As life speeded up at Ferrari-speed, the human brain took its own time to evolve. A part of Sona craved for the relaxed life of Shivagaon, but after spending a year there, she also knew that her tolerance level for relaxation was very low. She needed work, stress and speed in her life to teach her anew the value of rest and relaxation. But as this stress increased, Sona started losing her sleep. She did not want to take medication for her insomnia and was keen to explore alternative therapies. When Ammi suggested knitting, Sona grabbed it eagerly. As she watched the soft scarf increase in length, she felt a pleasant drowsiness creep over her. "I think I'll go up and sleep now Ammi," she said.

She climbed up the wooden staircase to the room on the other side of Nafisa's. Khaled resided in her old room now. This room was the second room meant for tenants. She was here only for a week. Nafisa and

Khaled were touring Madhya Pradesh as part of their project. Since Ammi had not been keeping well lately, Nafisa had asked Sona to come and stay with her during the time she was away. Shubhendu was in Kolkata, visiting his parents and Sona agreed to shift base to Ammi's place during Nafisa's absence. It was always a pleasure to be with this gracious old lady, listening to her tales from an earlier era and eating her fantastic food.

Sona hung on the balcony railing for a moment and breathed in the fragrance emanating from Ammi's old-fashioned garden. Ammi's garden was not very large, but in a city like Mumbai, even this little patch was like the Garden of Eden. There was a handkerchief lawn with well-maintained American grass. There was an elegant, short magnolia tree in a corner. A jasmine creeper that produced copious flowers throughout the year, scenting the surroundings with their subtle fragrance covered the brick boundary wall screening the house from the street. The pike-fence separating Ammi's plot from the neighbour had the *sankrant-vel* covering it from end to end. From November-end to March-end, this part of the garden brightened up with saffron-coloured flowers that added beauty to the neighbourhood. The flowerbeds had all the local plants, hardy and low-maintenance. "Hibiscus, mogra, kunda, and rajanigandha flowers that would have looked so beautiful," Sona thought, in her little puja ghar in Shivagaon. Ammi even had a tulsi plant in a big pot. It was ironical that though Ammi was not a Hindu, all the plants in her garden gave flowers beloved of Hindu deities. Ammi did not have much fascination for the imported plants that most of the plant nurseries seemed to be pushing their customers to buy. She scoured gardens of old friends and asked for cuttings of local plants from relatives visiting their villages. She had acquired after much effort a sapling of the *marwah* plant and she had enthusiastically told Sona that the little sapling had now grown into a respectable looking plant. It was a plant dear to Sona. It did not have much in the looks department. It was short, with small dark leaves. One could easily mistake it for a weed, but crush a sprig on your palm and it gave off an herbal scent of such magical power that one imagined a forest of delights peopled with little elves and fairies. Nafisa did not share this passion for gardening and so it was with Sona that Ammi mostly discussed the health and progress of her little garden. Sona knew all the plants in Ammi's garden and she had even added to the collection, knowing Ammi's liking for local plants.

The plants were not very clear in the darkness of the night. But Sona could distinguish their individual scents from the collective bouquet of fragrance. She looked up at the pretty little slice of moon that hung in the night sky. Sona felt calm and at ease with herself. The best part of staying with Ammi was that she always provided hot and fresh food at night. With her belly satisfied and her mind relaxed after her session of knitting, Sona allowed herself the luxury of lingering in the balcony for a while, taking in deep breaths of the garden scents and letting the night breeze cool her body. Finally, with a sigh she turned to go in. Sleep, that elusive stranger, would be her friend tonight.

It was just as she was drifting off to sleep that her mobile rang. Urgently and shrilly, it woke her up with a jerk. Her mind in turmoil, she picked up the mobile. Was Rajeev okay?

It was Sarita, her best girl pal from *News*. She was sounding frantic. "Did you see the late night news?"

"No, I was sleeping. What happened?"

There was silence. "Sona… your mother… Two hours back, someone shot her. Assailants are unknown. She was returning from an official function. They shot her in her car. She is critically injured. Bodyguard wounded. Sona…Sona…"

The mobile slipped from Sona's hands. Sarita's voice still on the mobile, repeating "Hello, hello" again and again was a messenger of darkness. Sona shut out the sound and clutched herself in fear. It could not be, it could not be. She was experiencing a nightmare. Soon morning would come and everything would be normal again. This could not be true. She drew the coverlet around her and rocked herself back and forth. This cannot be, this cannot be, she kept repeating like a mantra. She came to her senses with the sound of knocking on her door. She got up unsteadily to open it and Ammi quickly embraced her in a warm hug. Ammi brought her in and made her sit on the bed. Sarita had called up Ammi after the abrupt termination of the call with Sona. "Beti, beti", she said as she took Sona in her arms,

"Have courage child. She will come out of this. Your mother is a tough woman. Do not be afraid.

Shhh…" The old woman stroked her on the back and kept her in her embrace.

Sona whimpered but soon she disengaged herself and sat up. "Chibba! You devil! How could you do this! Ammi, I know who has done this. Chibba! He hates politicians. I hid my parentage when I had gone to interview him. He must have come to know and now he has taken revenge. Ammi, that man is a psychopath. He kills on a whim. Chibba! Chibba!" Sona shouted, "Why didn't you kill me instead of attacking my mother?" She turned a tear-stained face towards Ammi. "Ammi! My mother is paying for my deeds!"

"Sona, calm down… Calm down beti. Who told you that it was Chibba?"

"No one… But it *is* Chibba. It *is* Chibba who shot my mother."

In her mind, Sona saw Chibba's cruel lips move to order his men. He never soiled his hands. Only his henchmen did such killings. Sona saw them getting into a black Ambassador, two at the back and two in front armed with AK- 47 rifles. She saw the car lying in wait and silently following the white Ambassador that was taking her mother back to the bungalow on 7, Jaisingh Marg. She saw her mother's car stop at the red signal on Crescent Road and the black Ambassador stop next to it. A split second before the red turns to green, a burst of gunfire shatters the silence and the tinted glass of her mother's rolled-up car window and leaves her and her two bodyguards in a pool of blood. Seconds later, before the eye can blink, the black Ambassador has shot forward and disappeared into the dark anonymity of a stunned city. Sona saw all this so vividly that it was as though she had seen it all as an eye - witness. Her mother mowed down at a traffic signal while the killers made their getaway. "Chibba!" she screamed again, "I'll kill you."

She put her face in her hands and cried. Ammi let her cry, stroking her heaving back. Finally, Sona straightened.

"I've to go to Delhi Ammi…in the first available flight." She groped for her mobile that lay hidden in the bedclothes. Suddenly, her phone rang. It was Mr. Venugopal, Kamala Pradhan's faithful PA ringing up from Delhi. He sounded distressed. Sona's voice was ominously calm as she asked him the details. "Madam's car," Venugopal said, "had been ambushed just as it turned into Jaisingh Marg. One bodyguard was dead, the other injured. Madam was in the ICU at AIIMS. She had lost a lot of blood. The doctors refused to say anything more."

He continued, "Her meeting with the Japanese delegation had gone off so well this afternoon. Madam had been in such a good mood. She was to fly to Kathmandu tomorrow. I never thought… I never imagined…" Venugopal's thin voice cracked with emotion.

"Who were the gunmen?"

"Eh?" Venugopal's grief-filled chain of thoughts was broken. He groped to understand the steely voiced question, "Gunmen? Nobody has taken responsibility yet. Assailants are unknown. The police are investigating possibilities."

"Mr Venugopal, I'm taking the first available flight to Delhi. Will let you know as soon as I get a booking. Arrange for a pick-up for me from the airport."

"Eh…" Mr Venugopal said, his voice breaking.

"I am reaching Delhi tonight," Sona repeated, "Send someone to pick me up."

"Sonaji…oh, Sonaji, Madam is serious…" Mr Venugopal's voice cracked.

"Mr Venugopal," Sona's voice was surprisingly firm, "Pull yourself together. Do not give up so easily. I will be there soon. Together we will face the situation."

"Yes, yes Sonaji. Come as soon as you can. I am very much disturbed. Poor madam… oh, what has happened!" His voice trailed off.

He had been with Kamla Pradhan almost from the beginning of his career. As her fortunes soared, so did his. He came to her when he was a youngster, fresh out of college, wet behind the ears, eager to please. He made mistakes, but she would gently put him back on track. He proved his mettle and loyalty when Kamla Pradhan became the Chief Minister of Maharashtra. The press called him her little terrier by the door, but he never minded the jibes. He just did his duty, which was to look after Madam's interests. He worshipped the ground she walked on and she kept him on as her PA when she came to Delhi as a Union Minister. After years of working for her, he knew exactly what pleased Madam and what did not, what was okay with her and what was not. For this reason, he took it upon himself to vet the visitors who hounded her door daily. Protectively and possessively, he weeded out the undesirables, so vvthat Madam would not have to waste her precious time with riff-raff. Now someone had shot Madam. It was as though the bullet had hit Mr Venugopal himself. He was totally disoriented and was glad that Madam's daughter would be home to take control of things. His opinion of Sona reflected that of Kamla Pradhan's. He did not take the girl seriously. However, tonight she had sounded mature enough. Maybe she could be trusted after all to handle this ghastly affair.

Sona was frantically stuffing clothes into a suitcase. She readied her purse. All the important documents went into it. Ammi hovered at the door. "Pack woollens beti… Delhi will be cold. Maybe I should come with you. I hate to see you go all alone in a situation like this."

Sona came and put her arms around the old lady. She said, "I'll be fine Ammi. Just pray for me."

Her mind raced. Who could she call to accompany her? Rajeev was out of the country. Shubhendu was in Kolkata. Nafisa was in some village in Madhya Pradesh. Sarita had small kids to look after. She would have to go alone. Face it alone. She called up the airline and for the first time revealed her identity and relationship with Mother to book a seat on the VIP quota in the midnight flight to Delhi. Then she locked up her suitcase, zipped her purse and came out of her room. She hung for a moment over the railing of the balcony and surveyed the garden shrouded in darkness. The garden she had appreciated just a few hours before, now had hidden dangers in the dark corners. Evil lurked, silently waiting. For a moment Sona trembled. All the courage and strength that took her to Chibba's den was leaving her. She felt weak-kneed with anxiety. But she pulled herself together and hauled the suitcase downstairs. As she waited for the taxi that Ammi had called, she sipped the hot cup of sweet milk that Ammi pressed upon her. Ammi stroked her hair silently. The taxi arrived, and Sona bent down and touched the feet of the old woman, taking her permission to depart. Ammi stood at the gate and waved to her till the red tail lights of the taxi were swallowed up in the enveloping darkness.

19

As the plane soared over Mumbai, Sona looked emptily out of the window at the glittering city that spread below. Even at midnight, Mumbai did not sleep. Vehicles crept noiselessly like little lighted robots on the roads, the din of the city silenced by the ever-increasing distance between plane and land. City lights blinked. Buildings buzzed with electric lights and activity. The city twinkled like a diamond necklace, outshining the stars above. People were awake. They were working. Amazingly, the world went about its job, while Mother lay still. For Sona, it was impossible to imagine Mother motionless. In Sona's mind, Mother epitomized action. Even when Mother sat still, there was always a hum of activity around her. Mother could not leave this world abruptly like this! Without giving her any warning! There was a lot left unsaid. A lot remained unproved. She had to show Mother what she could achieve. How far she could go... Her journey had just begun. Without Mother, her achievements were null and void.

Her mother was not like other mothers, packing hot lunches in the school tiffin and preparing delicious and healthy tit-bits for after-school snacks. When Sona saw mothers of other girls in school, coming to pick them up and driving them for swimming and violin classes, she hated her mother for being different. When she saw mothers in advertisements cooking for their children and looking adoringly on while vthey ate what they had just prepared, Sona felt cheated. Why could Mother not be like a normal mother? The most enduring memory of Mother was of her disapproving look as she scanned Sona's report card. Mother's standards were too high. Sona gave up trying when she reached college. It was only after the Giridhar Dhir Award that Sona realised that she could be what Mother had always wanted her to be---an achiever. And now Mother was dying. Mother's vitality was the most striking quality about her. She was a doer. Sona had wanted her mother to be tender, loving and patient. The mother she got was active, purposeful and ambitious. She was also cold. Love was not in Mother's DNA.

And then out of nowhere Sona remembered the mid-week holiday that had been declared suddenly when she was in Boarding school. She remembered the parents and local guardians coming to pick up their wards. One by one they came and one by one her friends waved bye to her joyfully and left. She had called up Mother and informed her about this sudden holiday. Mother had advised her to read books in her room. She had an important meeting that day. Sona, eleven years of age, had banged the phone down. She had gone to her dorm and swallowing the tears that hurt her throat, had taken down her books to read. It was just before lunchtime that the hostel warden had come and told her that her mother was waiting for her downstairs. Sona had run down the corridor and hurried into the reception where Mther sat regally. Sona rushed into Mother's arms, the only time that she remembered being so demonstrative with her mother. Mother had put her arms around her. Sona still recalled the scent of Mother's soft cotton sari as she hugged her tight. "Come Sona, we'll go out for the day!" Mother said, and Sona, with shining eyes ran to her room to change into a nicer frock.

Mother had driven non-stop in her car to reach Panchgani before lunch. She had not attended the meeting after all, for once prioritising her only child above her work. That day, the few precious hours that Mother had spent with Sona were marked in Sona's memory. She enthusiastically showed Mother all her regular haunts. Then they had Sona's favourite Chinese food in the most famous roadside kiosk in the market, balancing on shaky stools and dealing with plastic cutlery as the world passed close by. They shopped a little in the quaint little hill town bazaar. The straw hat that Sona bought still hung from a hook in a room in Mother's bungalow in Delhi. Mother had clicked Sona's picture wearing the hat, the red ribbon around the hat rim quirkily blowing across her face and adding to the picture's breezy charm.

That day in Panchgani was a rare day of togetherness and tenderness. Mostly, Mother and Sona were on either side of the fence, so to speak. Not partners in life, but adversaries. Mother pushing and prodding, and Sona digging in her heels.

"What exactly do you want to do in life?" Mother had asked when Sona was in the final year of college.

Sona was good in languages and had taken Arts for graduation. She had expressed her desire to apply for the Rajmal Jain scholarship that would give her the opportunity to study journalism for a year at Oxford. How happy she had been when she had received the mail congratulating her on bagging the scholarship... Then, she had come to know through Mr Venugopal that Madam, who was then the Chief Minister of Maharashtra, had put in a word to the trustees for Sona. Sona had stormed into Mother's study that night. Mother and daughter had a major showdown and Sona, in a fury had dramatically torn the mail into shreds in front of mother's eyes. "How long Mother?" She had shouted, trembling with rage from head to toe, "How long are you going to interfere in my life like this? Will you never let me walk my path alone? Will none of my achievements be mine? Are only my failures my own? I do not want this scholarship. I do not want your favour. Let me achieve something by myself. I am not going to Oxford," and she had banged her way out of Mother's room. That was the beginning of the widening rift between the two. Mother had almost stopped talking to her after that. They lived in one house but avoided each other scrupulously. They ate separately and hardly shared a word with each other. Sona had applied for an internship at *News,* and had started working almost as soon as she had finished her year-long journalism course from a local Institute. The cold vibes between Mother and her continued. Then Sona met Rajeev.

Rajeev was hard working, disciplined, go-getting, ambitious...and he wanted her. Sona had never had a boyfriend before. Rajeev was the first guy she liked, who took interest in her. Sona had deep reservations about her looks. She felt short-changed by God when she compared herself to Mother. Mother was tall and fair complexioned. Sona was short and dark. Mother had authority stamped on her face. Sona looked hesitant and unsure. Mother was always supremely confident. Sona completely lacked confidence. Sona felt completely overshadowed in Mother's presence and this made her very sceptical about her desirability to the opposite sex. In the presence of guys, she always hung back, feeling shy and unsure. But Rajeev had stopped and looked beyond her ordinary physical persona. He stopped to look into her eyes and made her feel beautiful. "He was the first guy." she thought, "who looked at her, without looking over her shoulder for something better." Slowly, shyly, she allowed him to hold her hand and pull her close. When Mother said that love could wait, and that her career was more important, Sona made up her mind to marry. Who would take love-advice from a woman who never knew what love is!

Ironically, Mother inspired great confidence amongst the people of her constituency. As a leader, she was very effective. People were drawn to her, like bees to honey.

She radiated a kind of inner strength that attracted all. She was a natural leader, leading through example, showing genuine sympathy and kindness that promised a lifetime of loyalty. She was a people's person, effortlessly convincing the seniors within her party about her viewpoint and generously mentoring the juniors. She showed immense patience with the *janata janardan*, the common man, the public. It was only with her daughter that she became impatient and hard, expecting an excellence that was beyond the frail attempts of Sona. Though the two had only each other in the world, they lived together in uneasy co-existence. Mother's associates were vaguely aware of the friction between the two and naturally took the part of Madam. Sona had always been the difficult daughter who threw unnecessary tantrums and made Madam's hard life even harder. Foremost among these associates was Mr Venugopal. The two never got along. Just before boarding the flight and before taking off, Sona had tried Mr Venugopal's number but had been unable to get through. Sona wondered what arrangements Mr Venugopal had made to pick her up from the airport. He had sounded very distraught over the phone. It even seemed likely that he had not even registered what Sona was saying. She would try his number after landing, and if he did not pick up, she would straight away book a pre-paid taxi and go to AIIMS.

As the plane climbed higher and left the city lights far below, Sona closed her eyes and almost instantly fell asleep. She was woken up by someone shaking her by the shoulder. It was the stewardess, telling her that she should buckle her seat belt as they were now descending. Sona shook her head to ward off the sleep that enveloped her like a fog. She was still in the dream that had come to her vividly, leaving an aftertaste of unease.

In the dream she was eleven. She was sitting next to Mother, who was driving her car. They were going uphill, driving into the clouds. They climbed up and up and stopped in front of a red brick building, gracious and old. They got out and looked up at the building. The big double doors of the building opened and a woman came down the steps towards the car where Sona and Mother waited. As the woman, who was dressed in a billowy white dress, came closer, Sona saw that it was Nafisa. Nafisa stopped in front of Sona and smilingly handed her something. It was the keys of the car. Sona turned and saw that Mother was nowhere around. She was alone in that unfamiliar place. No Mother, no Nafisa. Sona looked at the keys in her hand and sat in the driver's seat. She started the ignition and drove the car out on the road. She did not take the road they had just taken. She turned into a different direction altogether. Just when Sona was trying to make sense of this weird dream, the stewardess woke her and left her without a sense of closure.

Sona ran a hand over her eyes and looked out of the window. The city lights were coming rapidly close. This time the lights were laid more systematically. The symmetry was more pronounced and regimented. The capital of India was lying in wait for Sona. She did not feel equal to the challenge at all. All she wanted was to hide behind Mother, as she always did in childhood. With a sudden and powerful impact, she realised the truth that Mother had been the roof over her head, the shield around her body, the guard at the door, the remote-controlled security cover that had emboldened her to do brave things. Things... that sometimes hurt Mother. And that roof had now collapsed. Sona was out in the open... Alone and vulnerable. There was no Mother to keep out the cold.

The plane finally taxied to a halt and Sona got up shakily. As they all came out to the exit, Sona's eyes clawed the sea of people who had come to pick up passengers. Most of the people were drivers who held up placards. 'Symantec for Arti'. 'Taj Palace for Mr Stephen Hall'. 'IBM for Mr Chandrashekhar'... where was Mr Venugopal? Sona's eyes looked for the familiar short and slight figure of Mother's loyal PA. But he was nowhere to be seen. Nor was there anybody holding a board or placard of her name. Mr Venugopal had not registered what she had instructed after all. Curse him! She dragged her cabin baggage on its wheels and stood there looking questioningly at the throng again when somebody tapped her on the shoulder. She turned and came face to face with a tall, distinguished looking man in Army uniform. He had a handsome angular face and salt and pepper hair. He shook her hand and introduced himself. "Ms Sona Jaykar I presume. Hello, I'm Brigadier Vikrant Singh."

20

"I've come to escort you to the hospital," he said.

She was surprised. "How did you recognise me?" she asked.

He looked down at her from his six foot height. "You look like her. When she was young," He said.

Just then, her mobile rang. It was Mr Venugopal. He said that Brig Vikrant Singh had volunteered to collect Sona from the airport. Sona followed the tall man out to the waiting Staff car and sat down mutely by his side at the back. The car drove through silent streets, lighted by street lamps. Spacious and deserted in the night chill, the surrounding scenery seemed sinister and strange, sending a stab of fear through her heart. She looked out quietly through the car window, feeling lost and alone.

"Don't be afraid. It will be alright!" Said a deep voice and she turned to look at the sharp profile of her co-passenger, his face and expressions hidden in shadow. She nodded.

At the hospital, she was greeted by Mr Venugopal. He took her straight to the ICU. She was allowed to only peep through the glass pane at the supine figure of Mother. How still she lay! Her face was white, as white as the hospital sheet covering her. Her eyes were shut. Tubes and drips were connected to her nose and hands, making her look heartbreakingly helpless. Mother and helpless! Sona turned away from the glass pane, unable to hold back her tears. It was early-early morning. Sona sat outside on the chair next to Mr Venugopal, who refused to leave. Brig Vikrant Singh paced up and down the corridor. When the doctor came on her rounds for the night shift, Sona went and spoke to her. Mother had been operated upon. Three bullets were removed from her stomach area. Fortunately, no vital organ was hit, but she had lost a lot of blood. She was still unconscious and the doctors were keeping their fingers crossed. If she was able to sail through the night without mishap, there was hope. But her chances of survival were still fifty-fifty. Sona's face showed clearly the strain she was going through. She walked up to the big glass window of the fifth floor corridor and looked down at the silent road below. Her mind felt empty. Her body felt tired. She turned and saw the tall figure of Brig Vikrant Singh striding towards her down the corridor. "Come Ms Jaykar, let me take you home. You look ready to drop. Mrs Pradhan is in safe hands. As it is, you will not be allowed to meet or talk to her until she gains consciousness. So, there's no point in staying here. Mr Venugopal is here... somebody will relieve him by nine in the morning. I will take you home and you can sleep for a while. You can come in the morning after freshening up." He took her by the elbow and she allowed him to lead her to the car.

The bungalow at '7, Jaisingh Marg,' was under extra security cover. Brig Vikrant Singh's staff car paused at the gate. He showed his identity, the sentry saluted him and the car entered the porch. The housekeeper was waiting under the dim electric bulb. He greeted them both, took her luggage and led them in. As they sat down on the big sofas in the drawing room, he brought them hot chocolate that he had kept ready to warm them on this cold night. They sipped the chocolate and looked at each other mutely. Then she gave him a wan smile. "Thank you Brigadier, for everything. Now, I'm home. I will be okay. I think you have done more than your duty."

To her great surprise, she saw his expression change. A look of pain shooting across his face, he said, "This is not duty…This is…" and he trailed off, his voice choking.

He got up to leave when they finished their drink and told her that he would come to take her to the hospital in the morning. He took her hand in his warm clasp as he turned to leave. "Try to sleep. You have a tough day tomorrow. Goodnight!" and he was gone, leaving her strangely bereft.

21

The next morning he was there to collect her. She quickly finished her eggs and toast. Ram Dayal brought her and Brig. Vikrant Singh excellently brewed tea. They had tea in silence. There had been no news from the hospital. Which was good. That meant that Mother had sailed through the night. Mr Venugopal was getting ready to leave his nightlong vigil, and take some much-needed rest. Sona would take his place.

At the hospital, Sona rushed to look at Mother through the glass pane. She was lying the same way as she had last night. "Get up Mother, move!" Sona said to the still figure. She came and sat down in the chair again. Brig. Vikrant Singh was talking to the doctor. He looked grave and serious. He came and sat by her. Sona gave him a long, searching look. He was restless and got up again to pace the corridor. Then he went to the glass pane and stood silently, looking quietly at the figure inside. Something in his expression made Sona's heart skip a beat. When he came and sat by her again, she turned to look at his face. "Brigadier," she said, "How well did you know my mother?"

The tall man turned his deeply tanned face towards her. "Your mother," he said, "was a good friend." Then he ran his hand over his face. "We were childhood friends. She was…" and he hesitated. "She is…special to me." He gave her a shadow of a smile. "We lost touch and then met again recently."

Sona felt a deep shiver, like a bolt of lightning course through her. It was as though a tectonic shift had taken place inside her head. All her memories, her beliefs, her thoughts about Mother did a complete turn-around. "Had she even known her mother? Her cold, distant mother…" She thought. Like all children, she harboured the sweet and completely false belief that her mother's life started only after the birth of her child. Mother had a history that preceded her, preceded Sona. Mother was a book that she had been able to read only half-way. Some vital chapters were missing. And the key to those chapters lay with this man.

"Tell me what Mother was like in school," Sona said, "She never spoke about her school days. And if she tried, I was never in a mood to listen."

Brig. Vikrant Singh gave a short laugh. His expression softened and he looked away, as though into the distant past. "Kamla was the Head Girl in school. She displayed exceptional leadership qualities even then. The Principal and staff listened to her feedback and the students were in awe of her. Everyone loved her, and I was one of her many admirers. I harboured some dreams about her, but in my heart of hearts felt unequal to her. Even then, I knew that she was marked for greater things.

The Kamla I knew was an extremely generous soul, feeling the sorrows of others as her own. And because she was so dynamic, she inspired confidence in those who lacked it." He looked at Sona, his eyes tired. "You are very lucky to have a mother like her."

They went down to the canteen to have tea and Sona listened as he spoke, filling in the gaps that lay in the complete portrait of Mother. He related anecdotes, smiled and laughed as he told about Mother's exploits. It was impossible to imagine Mother as a naughty teenager.

"You remember so much about Mother," Sona said, "Time has not faded those memories."

"Time has only made them clearer and sharper," he said, "Not a day goes when I don't remember her. My life would have been so different if she had been in it…" Brig. Vikrant Singh stopped. The two of them looked at each other across the table…connected by a strange kinship.

Just then, Sona's mobile buzzed. It was the doctor. Mother had gained consciousness. Sona and Brig Vikrant Singh raced up to the lift. Mother was still, but the tubes around her nose and mouth had been temporarily removed. Brig Vikrant Singh hung back as Sona rushed to Mother's side. Mother's eyes flickered with recognition. The nurse had told Sona not to tire her out. Mother was still in a medicated haze. The two held hands, their eyes speaking more than words. "Rajeev?" Mother asked huskily.

"He's reaching tonight from the US," Sona said, "Get well soon Mother. I need you. We all need you." She turned and gestured towards the glass pane. The door opened and Brig Vikrant Singh walked in. Kamla Pradhan's eyes lit up. He came towards the bed. Sona quietly slipped out of the door, tears falling down her cheeks.

Before long the Brig joined her. He was trying hard to hold back his tears. "I think we should go back home now. She has drifted back into unconsciousness. The doctor feels that she is fighting back, showing improvement. Her condition has stabilised. All we can do is wait and watch. You look exhausted. I'll take you home."

Back home, as usual Ram Dayal had kept hot chocolate ready. They sat and sipped it quietly, sitting in the drawing room, the hot liquid bringing life back to their cold spirits. When Brig. Vikrant got up to leave, Sona put up a timid hand to his sleeve. "Please don't go. Stay. The guest room is ready. I am afraid to be alone tonight."

The tall, hardy man, who had not turned back those many years ago when someone had called to him, now stopped and looked into the troubled eyes of the young woman. He patted her hand and nodded.

He made a few phone calls. They sat and watched the news on TV. Then came the news flash. Mother's attackers had been identified. Qader Ilahi's gang had taken responsibility. So, it was not Chibba after all! A part of Sona's mind relaxed in the knowledge that Mother's assailant was not the man who had called her 'sister'. Qader Ilahi was reputed to be out of the country, hiding in some neighbouring country. Mother had played a big role in liquidating his gang during her tenure as Maharashtra's CM. She had the full support of the then brave and dynamic Commissioner of Police, who agreed that in finishing the Qader Ilahi gang lay the safety and security of Mumbai. Through countless encounters and ambushes, the gang was declared to be over, its spine broken. But Qader Ilahi managed to flee. And now, he had reared his head by sending a brutal message of revenge through this attack on Mother.

Sona and Brig Vikrant Singh followed the news on several channels. Mother was in the headlines again. Every channel had eminent panellists discussing the attack on the Union Minister. Sona slumped in her chair, numb with frustration and sorrow. She shut her ears to the cacophony. Brig Vikrant Singh looked at her. His face mirrored her expressions. He put off the TV and the two got up. She wished him good night and went into her room with a heavy heart, for a night of troubled sleep.

It was around three in the early-early morning when there was a call from the hospital. Mother was slipping away. It was better if Sona came to the hospital immediately. Brig Vikrant Singh drove in utter silence. Only the clenching and unclenching of his jaw indicated the stress he was going through. The car speeded through deserted streets. Sona kept a tight leash over her emotions.

In the hospital, Dr Bhattacharya, the Chief Surgeon personally greeted them. It was all over. Mother had infact passed away when the phone call had been made. She just took a deep breath and never took another breath again. Sona went over to Mother's body. Body?? That was not a body! It was her mother. A mother with whom she shared blood and DNA and genes and memories and feuds and love and anger and hatred and…Sona put her head near her dead mother's face and cried as though her heart would break.

Somebody came and patted her back. She turned and fell into the tight embrace of Brig. Vikrant Singh. She cried, and their tears mixed. He raised her face up then and whispered, "Control yourself now Sona. We will cry later." She swallowed her tears and gulped her sobs away.

Funeral arrangements were handled by the Party functionaries. Sona signed some documents and arrangements were made to shift Mother's body to '7, Jaisingh Marg'. Sona was in a daze, but throughout she felt the comforting presence of Brig. Vikrant Singh by her side. Rajeev had arrived and was waiting at '7, Jaisingh Marg', looking jet-lagged and bewildered. Sona reached Mother's official bungalow and had a meeting with the Party functionaries. It was decided that Mother's body would be kept in state in the hall for people to pay their last respects. Mother had been a popular and beloved leader. The funeral would take place the next day. Then, Sona just locked away her emotions and started working on auto. She directed Ram Dayal to make the necessary arrangements for the final darshan. With Mr Venugopal she discussed about the extra security arrangements. With the party functionaries she went over some points before briefing the media. She went inside and outside, passing Mother's body several times. Around afternoon, as she was rushing off to the kitchen, she felt someone drag her down to sit. A glass of nimbu-pani was thrust into her hands. As though in a haze, she saw Brig. Vikrant Singh raise the glass to her lips. She took the glass and sat down. He sat down beside her and put his arms around her shoulder. She leaned against him and he said, "Drink this! You've not had anything since morning." She sipped the cool nimbu-pani like an obedient child.

The steady stream of mourners continued. They filed past the flower-bedecked body of Mother. So serene she looked in death! She looked more beautiful than in life... Peaceful. The flowers and the incense smoke made the atmosphere strangely spiritual. For a while, Sona just sat next to Mother, blankly accepting the condolences of the people who came. But in her mind she was with Mother, running down the slope of her Panchgani boarding school with her, laughing, as Mother ran ahead in her white cotton sari. She finally caught up with Mother, and then they both held hands and ran down the slope together. Probably the last time that they held hands so intimately. Sona reached out and touched Mother's hand. It was cold. It was stiff. Mother was not there. She was gone. Forever.

Tears threatened to spill, but Sona swallowed them hurriedly. From the corner of her eye, she saw Rajeev at the other end of the hall. He was talking on his mobile. Sona searched the room, but the familiar figure of Brig. Vikrant Singh could not be seen. She leaned back with a sigh.

By eight at night, the crowd had ebbed. The security at the gate forbade any more visitors. It was just Rajeev and Sona now in the big bungalow. Sona slept badly, disturbed by the gentle snores of Rajeev. Day was breaking tentatively and shyly when Sona decided to get up and make herself a cup of tea. Holding a mug of her special brand of strong ginger tea Sona strolled into Mother's bedroom. Four nights ago, Mother had slept here. Her presence still pervaded the air in the room. Her slippers peeped from under the bed. The book she was reading lay spread-eagled on the bed. The sari she had worn last lay neatly folded on the rack next to the dressing table. Mother had always been neat and tidy. Her bedroom was a testimony to her neatness fetish. Sona drew away the curtains and looked out at the spacious lawn. It lay green and dew-wet. This was Mother's favourite time of day...early morning. By this time yesterday, Mother was gone. Forever taking away with her unspoken secrets and the hand of protection over Sona's head that Sona found so heavy to bear. "Goodbye Mother!" Sona whispered, "Rest in peace!"

Sona dressed then and got ready for a difficult day. She conducted herself like an actor before the glare of the media. She followed Mother's hearse in a car, seated between Rajeev and Brig. Vikrant Singh. At the cremation, she lit Mother's funeral pyre and watched the flames consume the logs in a final lick of annihilation. As the flames touched the body, she gave a great sob. Rajeev touched her arm but she turned and hid her face in Brig. Vikrant Singh's chest. He held her close against his hard body, as she let her sobs come unabated. The image was captured shamelessly by the hungry media. Their pictures were telecast across thousands of homes across the country. Forever and ever, Sona Jaykar would now be Mrs Kamla Pradhan's daughter.

Mother had left the world as flamboyantly as she had lived in it. In a way, this was the only kind of death befitting her. Not for her a quiet death in bed... In anonymous retirement ... Her body old and bent... And her name a dim memory in people's minds. She had died while she was still on duty, for the service of the people, a leader born to the manner. All through her life, she had thrived on publicity. The Press was her friend and she had a wonderful rapport with the media. After her death, they did not fail her. She and the manner of her death was the major story in all the magazines and newspapers. "Yes," thought Sona, "this was the way to go."

PART-II

22

Sona leaned back in her chair and stretched. It was late. She was the only one left in the office. It was almost nine. But putting in long hours at work had become a habit with Sona. For the past one month, since she was asked by Mr Jeevan Prabhu, the proprietor of Swan Publishing, to become the founder editor of the new magazine launched by Swan, Sona had been working extra hard. *Street* was a magazine aimed at young people. It had been Mr. Jeevan Prabhu's dream for a long time. Two months ago, he had summoned Sona for a meeting and discussed the idea with her. She enthusiastically offered suggestions and the next day, he had offered her the editorship of the magazine. It was a challenging task. But he offered her full support and no interference. "Choose your team, Sona," he said, "Implement the ideas that you so enthusiastically put forward yesterday. I will not spare any expenses. But I want this magazine to capture this niche market. I am sure you can do it. You are young and have your finger on the pulse of the young populace. I could see that when I spoke to you yesterday. Remember, there are others who are senior than you in the establishment, but I have always gone with my gut feeling. I feel you are right for the job."

As though in a daze she had got up and shaken his hand. When the old man spoke, it was impossible to deny him anything. It was only later that she realised the extent of work she had committed herself to. She had to start the magazine from scratch, build a team, hammer out a strategy and give *Street* a special look and flavour. It was not as easy as it had seemed initially and staying late in office became almost a daily affair.

The good part was that her salary had increased dramatically. Also, as sole heir of Mother's property and assets, she was now independently wealthy. She had moved out of her rented apartment and shifted into '1, Sagar Apartments', Mother's sea-facing apartment that she had scorned when she had first shifted base to Mumbai.

It would soon be a year since Mother passed away. A year of mourning and getting to know a mother whom she had always strained against. With Mother's death went also Sona's grievances against her. As Sona reconciled with her dead Mother, her antipathy to '1, Sagar Apartments' waned. She shifted into this dream apartment that Mother was always talking of retiring to.

With '1, Sagar Apartments', Sona inherited also Shevanti and Raghu, the couple who stayed in the servant quarters of the apartment and who were the caretakers of this posh property. Mother had acquired this beautifully located apartment when she was the CM of Maharashtra. At that time, she was living in the appointment house of the CM and later she shifted to Delhi and into '7, Jaisingh Marg'. '1, Sagar Apartments' remained unoccupied. It was

Mother's haven, the dream house that she always talked about. She had furnished it lovingly with key furniture pieces. Chief among them was a rocking chair that she had inherited from her parents' house. A couple of paintings that her father had done hung in the drawing room and all over the place were black and white photographs of Sona. Sona as a baby, Sona as a toddler, Sona in Mother's arms, Sona dressed primly in her school uniform, Sona on her wedding day. Sona, Sona, Sona...'1, Sagar Apartments' was Mother's gift to Sona, and Sona had broken her heart when she refused to shift into the place when she came to Mumbai. At that time, '1, Sagar Apartments' had intimidated Sona. It was less a sanctuary and more a spider's web. Struggling to maintain her own centre of gravity and individuality, the confines of '1, Sagar Apartments' had seemed claustrophobic and asphyxiating. Sona had wished to escape the clutches of Mother and that would have been impossible if she had lived in '1, Sagar Apartments'.

But now, Sona had made her peace with Mother. A big part in this journey of healing and reconciliation was played by Brig. Vikrant Singh. After Mother's dramatic death and highly publicized funeral, Brig Vikrant Singh became the person Sona felt closest to. He had known Mother as a pig-tailed teenager. He knew a part of Mother that Sona never would. As Sona realised gradually and enviously, he had loved Mother truly and completely. This fact Sona digested slowly and painfully. Mother had savoured a love that is bestowed to very few... Denied to many... Denied even to Sona. Sona's thoughts drifted to Rajeev. *Geeta*

Engineering Works was well on its feet. But Rajeev showed no signs of slowing down. He continued with his punishing schedule. His trips abroad and within India went on unabated. He was talking of expansion now, and diversifying into other kinds of manufacturing as a hedge for sudden recession in one sector. "Workaholism, thy name is Rajeev!" sighed Sona, as she switched off the computer monitor and got up to leave.

As she reversed the car out of the Swan House parking and hit the main road, she speculated about what Shevanti had prepared for dinner. What a comfort Shevanti was! Unlike countless working women, Sona did not have to agonise about what and how to prepare meals morning, afternoon and evening. Sona again thanked Mother mentally for this blessing. Shevanti was Mother's find. When she was CM of Maharashtra, she had visited one of the drought-affected areas. There, during a tour of the local orphanage, some social workers had pointed to the thin, dark child looking utterly lost and woebegone. Shevanti had lost her farmer parents to starvation and poverty. Something in the child's appearance captured her attention and she had stopped and made many enquiries about her. She told the authorities that she was sponsoring the child's education and upkeep and that she would be making constant enquiries about her. Thus, Shevanti studied till the tenth standard, dutifully writing letters to her guardian every Sunday. When she turned eighteen, Mother got her married to a suitable young man, who was working in a factory in Mumbai. She offered them the servant quarters as accommodation in return for taking care of the apartment. In space-crunched Mumbai, this was a gift from the gods and this is how Shevanti and Raghu came to be a part of '1, Sagar Apartments'. They both were Mother's true supporters. Shevanti was devastated with Mother's death and with logic peculiar to her own brand of loyalty, shifted her love smoothly from Mother to her daughter.

Shevanti opened the door in a flurry. "Again you are late Tai," she scolded, "I've made your favourite fried karela for dinner. Come quickly to the dining table. I'll make hot rotis for you."

Sona smiled and entered as Shevanti took her bag from her. "You make me feel like a traditional Indian husband Shevanti!" But the jest was lost on Shevanti, who hurried away to keep the bag and make hot rotis.

As she polished off the second roti, Sona got a call from Rajeev. He was making his duty call of the day. "Mother is coming to India for a month. Try to take some days off from work during that time. If we cannot give her a grandchild, at least we can give her our time." He sounded censorious. Sona knew all about Rajeev's bucket list. This grandchild bit always came up whenever Rajeev's mother was mentioned. Sona sighed and promised to keep it in mind. As she kept down the phone, she thought of the Geeta of *Geeta Engineering Works*. Frankly, Sona hardly knew her. She knew her only as a trans-Atlantic voice. A petite bird-like woman, she looked fragile and delicate like a porcelain doll. She was unfortunate to lose her husband so early in life. But she was fortunate to get two sons like Arjun and Rajeev. They both worshipped the very ground their mother stepped on and it was a matter of constant competition between them to grab her attention and affection. When Rajeev was with his mother, the two were in a circle of love that excluded Sona. And Sona knew that the special place in Rajeev's heart was reserved for his mother. For that reason, Sona was careful to never say anything against her mother-in-law. Not that she had anything against the delicately beautiful woman. She was a total contrast to Mother. Mother gave protection to others. She inspired confidence and loyalty in people. Geeta Jaykar inspired the protective instinct in others. She looked vulnerable and lost... Needy and defenceless. From childhood, her two sons had fallen into a pattern. Their role was that of protector. Their mother needed their protection. Sona thought of her own mother. She felt proud of Mother... A born leader! No wonder her life never followed the usual trajectory chalked out for average Indian girls. But it made her so demanding and hard with her own child. A child who desperately wanted tenderness was offered bitter doses of duty and ambition. "Love can make us so unbending sometimes," Sona thought.

As Shevanti cleared the dishes and cleaned the kitchen for the night, Sona switched on the TV for the news. The same old noisy panel discussions and debates were going on, on every news channel. She yawned. Shevanti bid her goodnight and Sona switched off the TV. As she tucked into bed and picked up the book by her bedside, her mobile rang. It was Brig Vikrant Singh. In her mind, Sona always called him 'the Brigadier', but as they had bid farewell to each other at Delhi airport after Mother's funeral, Brig. Vikrant Singh had taken Sona's hand and said, "Call me VS! Brigadier is too formal." VS was how all his NDA batch mates called him and now Sona called him that too.

Next month would be Mother's first death anniversary. "We should meet then", he said. Sona promised to see how to manage a trip to Delhi, where he was currently posted.

As Sona kept down the phone, a new idea struck Sona. The turmoil of the past few months had made her shelve her book on the mystery thriller she had begun. But now, she started to toy with the idea of writing Mother's biography. Mother's early life lay like a newly made film in the memory of Brig Vikrant Singh. She would bounce off this idea with him and see how it could be worked upon. Wondering about this new project, Sona nodded off, a smile on her lips.

23

"Rajeev thinks that it is quite easy for me to get away as and when I want… That the editorship of *Street* is a cakewalk, and that my job is not as critical as his." Sona was venting to Nafisa. The two were having coffee at the café close to Sona's office. It was lunchtime and they were enjoying their coffee and scones.

"That's not true Sona," Nafisa, who liked Rajeev, said, "Give the guy some credit. For somebody who was brought up the traditional way, Rajeev gives you a lot of space. But his mother is his weak point. He wants her to feel that his life is going just perfectly well, which obviously means that he needs your presence. He wants your cooperation in this, and Sona, what is the harm is stretching yourself a bit as far as this issue is concerned? He has never crossed you on other things has he? Sometimes, one has to put aside one's own feelings for others. And he is not even an 'other'. He is your husband."

"And so speaks a woman who is living life on exactly her own terms!" Sona exclaimed. It was a matter of enduring surprise to Sona that Nafisa's relationship with Khaled had not put even a blemish on Nafisa's spotless reputation. The respect she received as a scholar and academician remained unchallenged. Otherwise, for a woman, and a successful woman at that, the first area to be attacked was her character.

And academia was notorious for envious people with loose tongues. Nafisa was beautiful, successful and young. She was a soft target. Yet, the very openness with which she led her life just dispelled all the arrows of attack. The fact that she and Khaled were a couple was known to all, even to her students. Yet it did nothing to lessen their respect for her. Her dignified demeanour, her genuine scholarship and her brave and bold acknowledgement of her offbeat life choices covered her with an impregnable sheath of protection, which even the most malicious gossip mongers could not penetrate.

"What does the future hold for Khaled and you?" Sona asked, and Nafisa's face fell as she answered, '"Frankly, I don't know! I am just hoping that something will work out. Don't ask me what!"

"Rajeev's mum arrives in India next week," Sona said, changing the topic, "I'll be going to receive her at Mumbai International airport and then Rajeev is sending the car which will take her to Shivagaon. I will be going to Shivagaon on the week following her arrival. That is what has cheesed off Rajeev. He wanted me to be well entrenched in Shivagaon before his mum's arrival to give an impression of domestic conviviality. But I just can't get away next week. Rajeev na…!" Sona pouted.

Nafisa looked at her closely, and then as if a new thought had struck her asked suddenly, "Sona! Have you met someone recently?"

Sona started so violently that her hand shook and drops of coffee spilled on the table. She dabbed it hurriedly and said, "Whatever gave you this ri-di-culous idea?!"

"Nothing specific," Nafisa shrugged, and took a sip of her coffee, "Just an idea that occurred to me," and she looked speculatively at Sona over the rim of her coffee cup. This meeting between Nafisa and Sona had taken place after much planning and juggling of schedules on both their parts. Sona's Sundays were eaten up with office work and Nafisa had other plans with Khaled. That left only weekdays and it was sometimes the traffic, sometimes their work schedules, sometimes their inclination that came in the way. Though they kept in touch over the phone, this face-to-face meeting was taking place after a long time and that too because of effort on Nafisa's part. Sona was cutting herself off from old friends and Nafisa thought that there had to be a reason for it. Sona's heart was being pulled elsewhere. Where? Nafisa speculated further.

As the two friends took leave of each other and Sona walked into the Swan House building, her mobile pinged. A message from VS! "Am coming to Mumbai on work next Wednesday...we can meet."

Sona's spirits sank. "Am leaving for Shivagaon on Wednesday..." she typed, "MIL duty!"

There was a long pause and then the screen flashed... "Duty first!"

As Sona went about her work the whole of the week, she felt restless and tired. She snapped unnecessarily at colleagues and was uncommunicative with Shevanti. She spoke in monosyllables with her mother-in-law over the phone, forgetting to put on the over-chirpy voice that she always adopted while speaking with her. With Rajeev she spoke curtly, forcing him to come out of his self-absorbed stupor to ask, "What's wrong Sona? Has something happened?"

But even Sona did not know why she was off-colour. All she knew was that this vibrant, technicolour world had suddenly become black and white.

24

The tall man walked out of the Arrivals gate at Mumbai airport with long strides, wheeling his bag behind him. People made way for him automatically, such was the authority in his bearing. He walked briskly, not looking here or there. Just as he emerged out of the air-conditioned confines of the building into the mugginess of a Mumbai evening, a figure in the distance caught his eye. He stopped and his heart lurched. "Kamla?" He mouthed in disbelief. The woman in the white sari saw him at that moment and came towards him. In an instant, Brigadier Vikrant Singh had gathered her in his arms. "Sona?" he said in a delighted whisper, "You came? What about 'duty first'?"

Sona looked up at him. "I am not my mother VS!"

With school-boyish enthusiasm, Brig Vikrant Singh held her hand as they walked out to the car parking. Sona reversed her compact SUV in a graceful arc and hit the main road within minutes. Brig Vikrant Singh eased his long legs in the passenger seat and looked at her with amused pride.

"What?" Sona laughed, "Why are you looking at me like that?"

"Just appreciating the way you drive. How well you drive!"

"Surprised? That a woman can drive well?"

"Not at all!" said he, "Remember, I knew your mother. What an excellent driver she was!"

"You are coming to my place for dinner now. We will not get time otherwise. I am leaving for Shivagaon tomorrow. I cannot postpone it any longer now... Rajeev is already annoyed with me for postponing it by a day."

"Whatever you say Ma'am," Brigadier Vikrant Singh said, "You are the boss."

They entered '1, Sagar Apartments' and were greeted with the welcome aroma of delectable food being prepared in the kitchen. Shevanti was preparing her famous chicken. Brig Vikrant Singh was a foodie, though one would not guess that, looking at his washboard flat stomach.

Sona chattered ceaselessly. They had kept up a lively correspondence after they parted at Delhi. It was an immediate connect between the two. Though this was their first meeting after they said farewell on a cold foggy Delhi evening eight months ago, their digital communication had uncovered layers of their personality to each other that made them feel that they were old friends. Brigadier Vikrant Singh was a paratrooper, part of the elite Indian Army force, he had been the Services Squash champion in his younger days and for a brief while was the National champion. He had commanded key Units in field areas and had supervised anti-terrorist operations in J&K that had brought him the AVSM. In spite of all this he was modest, never bragging. Yet, there was an air about him that made him stand apart from the milling crowd. They sat together in the drawing room. Sona with a glass of red wine, and Brigadier Vikrant Singh with a glass of lime and soda. He was a strict teetotaller, keeping away from alcohol at all times.

"Swaroop has been talking of migrating to Canada," he said suddenly.

Sona looked at him askance. "What? Why this sudden whim?"

"It is not sudden. It started soon after Kamla's assassination. Her brother has migrated there and her parents will soon be joining him. She says that if we migrate now, we would be able to settle down there before we are too old. She thinks that Canada will offer our two kids better opportunities."

"But what about your career? You are going great guns. You will go far. You are a born Army man. I am surprised that she did not think of your career. She is a fauji's daughter too."

"Something is bothering her," Brigadier Vikrant Singh said, "She wants to take me away from India."

"And do you also want that?" Sona asked.

Brigadier Vikrant Singh looked at her with his piercing dark eyes. "I'll never quit the Army. Never leave India."

"Then Swaroop will leave you…"

"That will be her choice," he said.

They looked at each other silently and then the Brigadier shrugged and took a sip of his drink. Sona was about to say something when her mobile shrilled. It was Rajeev. "Where are you?" he snapped.

"I'm at home," Sona said, "Brigadier Vikrant Singh has come for dinner. You met him at Delhi…"

"What is that man doing there?"

Sona felt as though she had been slapped. "Excuse me…" she said to Brigadier Vikrant Singh and rushed inside to her bedroom.

"What did you just say?" she said sharply, her chest heaving, "His name is Brigadier Vikrant Singh. He is a highly decorated soldier of the Indian Army. A man who puts duty before self. He was a close friend of my mother. He was…"

"Your mother's lover!" Rajeev hissed.

Sona let this sink in. "Yes", she said deliberately, "and never was there a couple more suited for each other. More above-average, more elevated and exalted than the common riff-raff who make up the bulk of humanity. You watch your words Rajeev! I will not have my close friends denigrated like this. As for your dear mother… rest assured, I will be taking the evening train to Shivagaon tomorrow after putting in a full day in office. I will reach tomorrow by eight in the night. If this call was about confirming my plan, then don't worry, I will be there!"

With that, Sona switched off her mobile and taking a deep breath came out to the drawing room.

Brigadier Vikrant Singh looked at her searchingly. "Hubby angry?" He asked, "You look upset."

"It is nothing…" and Sona forced a smile, "Let me go and see about the dinner." She disappeared into the kitchen where Shevanti was bustling about busily.

"Just fifteen minutes more Tai," Shevanti said.

Sona poured herself a generous amount of red wine and came out to the drawing room. Brigadier Vikrant Singh looked at her glass and shook his head. "Not good, my girl. Do you always drink more when you are upset?"

Sona came and sat next to him on the sofa. Tears shone in her eyes. "Why is life so complicated?"

"Life is simple," the Brigadier said, patting her hand, "We complicate it by over-analysing it!"

They had a satisfying meal, with Shevanti bringing in hot rotis. Brigadier Vikrant Singh relished each morsel and praised Shevanti, bringing a smile to her dark face. Sona told him about her idea of writing Mother's biography and got his enthusiastic approval and support. It was late in the night when he got up, putting his coffee cup on the centre table as Sona called for a cab to take him to the place where he was putting up. As he got up to leave, Sona touched his arm. "Thank you for being in my life VS!"

Brigadier Vikrant Singh smiled ruefully, patted her cheek and was gone.

25

The lift doors were about to close when Sona entered Swan House the next morning. She rushed towards it and wedged a foot in, forcing it to open before squeezing herself inside the lift. Once inside, she came face to face with Shubhendu. "Hi!" she said sheepishly. He just smiled and tilted his head. He pressed the '3' button and Sona pressed '5'.

"How's the Editor of *Street*?" he asked.

"Fine," she said, reddening under an implied taunt, "And how's the Assistant-Editor of *News*?"

"Just as before…no change!"

They looked at each other mutely. After returning from Delhi following her mother's assassination, Shubhendu had felt a change in Sona. She never called him up now and their Sunday get-togethers had stopped completely. Sona said that she was preoccupied with work, but Shubhendu felt that she was avoiding him. There was some other reason.

"Sona," he said, "you've met someone, haven't you?"

The lift doors opened. They had reached the third floor. Sona kept quiet. Shubhendu got out of the lift and the two kept looking at each other until the door closed and travelled up, taking Sona to the top floor. Meeting Shubhendu now-a-days always left Sona a little disturbed. She scratched at an imaginary itch on her back and entered her office with a frown on her forehead.

Since she was leaving office at four-thirty to catch the five o'clock train to Shivagaon, she had to hurry through the jobs she had lined up for the day. This encounter with Shubhendu kept irritating her throughout the day. Was she really so transparent? Nafisa had asked her the same question too. But why were they asking her this, when there was nobody special in her life? She had a marriage, lukewarm though it was, and so had no business to be meeting anyone 'special'. Why were these two troubling her with unnecessary questions!

It was five in the evening. As she settled into her train seat with a book in her hand, she wondered what the scene would be like in Shivagaon. She had not spoken to Rajeev after last night's spat. It was unlikely that he would pick a fight with her in the presence of his mother, yet Sona's heart fluttered with dread. She was rarely rude with Rajeev. They were rarely rude with each other. Rajeev had impeccable manners and was brought up to address everybody as 'aap', including his wife. Last night's behaviour was atypical. Why this animosity towards Brigadier Vikrant Singh? He sounded jealous. He had never shown jealousy when Sona had told him that she spent every Sunday at Shubhendu's place. Infact, he had laughed indulgently. Thus, this outburst from him had taken her by surprise. Why be jealous of Brigadier Vikrant Singh?

Sona shook her head and tried to concentrate on her book. But the words just danced in front of her eyes. As the train picked up speed, Sona's eyes closed. She was soooo tired. Why did people trouble her with unnecessary questions? Why did they not leave her in peace? It was a blank sleep, dreamless...where her mind had only blocks of colours. Slate, grey, black, brown, olive green...

She awoke with a jerk, as though with a sixth sense. She looked out of the window, but the landscape outside was an even dry expanse typical of rural Maharashtra. She hurriedly asked her co-passenger, "Have we passed Nasrapur?"

"No," he said, "we are nearing it."

Sona pressed her face against the window to take in the approaching scenery. She was going to Shivagaon after a long gap. After Mother's assassination, it was as if her life and life's priorities just changed. Nothing seemed as it was before. For weeks after that, months, she was numb emotionally. "Chalo, bikharne dete hai zindagi ko ab! / sambhaalne ki bhi toh ek hadd hoti hai!" These words from an obscure Urdu sher that she had come across somewhere just fitted her mood. She scribbled it down and it lingered in her mind like the strong incense scent that wafted over from the dargah across her office. She was tired of holding on. Something was slipping out of her hand, like sand, and she could do nothing to ebb the flow. She did not have the strength.

Nasrapur was approaching. She peeped out, looking for Savitri and her brood. The Station Master's house lay shuttered and silent. There was no sign of life. No Savitri! No hustle and bustle of Sonya and Saguna. Sona felt a pang. She was half hoping that here at least things would be as expected. The train stopped for a short while at Nasrapur. Sona saw the stationmaster hurrying towards the engine. Was it her imagination or was it true that he had aged considerably in the past few months? He looked drawn and haggard and his gait was like that of an old man. "Oh God!" Sona thought, "What had happened to Savitri?"

Shivagaon came soon after. The car and driver were waiting for her. It was almost eight when the car turned inside the gate. The garden and porch lights were on. So were the lights inside. Dara was sitting in his usual place in the porch. He gave a joyous bark and bounded towards the car. He was all over her as she stepped out of the car, his tongue hanging out and tail wagging furiously. Yes, at least Dara never held a grudge against her. She accepted the big dog's boisterous welcome and then they both headed towards the house, as the driver took out her luggage and followed. She entered the hall and a cosy family picture greeted her eyes. Her fragile and beautiful mother-in-law was seated at the dining table. Next to her sat Preeti, looking comfortable and very much at home. She was slicing apples and saying something laughingly to Rajeev who sat across, an indulgent smile on his face. They all looked up as Sona entered, Dara announcing their arrival noisily. Preeti got up hastily and Rajeev came towards her. Her mother-in-law smiled faintly and Sona went towards her, bowing down to touch her feet and take her blessings.

She looked at Rajeev, who smiled but stood where he was.

"Good evening madam," Preeti said effusively, "Shall I make a cup of tea for you?"

"Relax Preeti!" Sona said sweetly, "You are our guest here. I will tell Champabai to make it. She knows exactly how I like it."

Preeti subsided in her chair, her face red.

"Preeti is not exactly a guest Sona," Rajeev said, after an awkward pause, "She is like a member of the family. She has been coming here daily since Mummy's arrival, giving her company and helping her know the town better. She was just being courteous."

"Well, I should thank her then! I can see how enjoyable her company is!"

The catty words were out of her mouth before she could stop them. Sona turned towards the kitchen, biting her tongue. Why was she saying such things? What devil was making her behave like this in front of her saintly mother-in-law? What was happening to her? Things were falling apart. The centre could not hold.

"Chalo, bikharne dete hai zindagi ko ab!

Sambhaalne ki bhi ek hadd hoti hai!"

In the kitchen, Champabai was furiously whirring the mixer, preparing the wet masala for the chicken. Sona gave her a watery smile and bent to take out the tea utensil. As she reached out for a cup, it was gently taken away. "Let me help madam," Preeti said softly, "We'd all like a cup each."

"I'm sorry Preeti," Sona said, allowing her to take it away, "That was mean of me."

"It is okay, madam," Preeti said, briskly measuring out the water by the cupful, "You are just tired."

26

Both Rajeev and Sona did not refer to last night's spat. It was as though both had pressed the 'delete' button on the episode. Sona had taken five days off from work. Those five days she spent with her mother-in-law, taking her on outings and little shopping expeditions. On the second day, just before dinner, her mother-in-law came down with a leather jewellery box. Very ceremoniously, she opened it and took out a diamond jewellery set. She clasped the necklace on Sona's neck, helped her to wear the bracelet and told her to wear the diamond danglers.

"Mummyji, it is too expensive!" Sona exclaimed.

"It is nothing for my bahu," her mother-in-law said, "You are the izzat of the Jaykar family. You hold its honour in your hand. Bas beti, if you have had your fill of your career now, just come home and take care of my son and his house. I am waiting for news of a grandchild. Arjun already has two kids. You should start a family soon now. Rajeev will be a very good father." She looked affectionately at her son. Sona looked at Rajeev and he looked back at her. Geeta Jaykar snapped the box shut in a decisive way and Sona stood there mutely, like a mannequin in the middle of the room, the jewels glittering on her body…

Rajeev went back to his routine after Sona's arrival and continued with his usual factory hours.

He was planning to take his mother to her hometown after Sona went back to Mumbai. He would be taking a week off from work then, so that his mother could spend time with her brother, cousins and extended family. Then he would return to Shivagaon and she would follow a week later. After spending another week in Shivagaon, she would return to the US. As long as Sona was in Shivagaon, she was the devoted daughter-in-law and wife. This time around, she did not interfere with the way Champabai and Ganpat were managing the affairs. "Why disrupt their routine," she thought, "when I would be gone in a few days? Let the house chug along the way they deem best."

On the last night before her departure to Mumbai, they had organised a party at home. Preeti turned up two hours before the scheduled time. "Rajeev sir insisted that I should be here to assist and help you," she said, "Besides, you are leaving early morning tomorrow. You need to get yourself organised. Leave the running around and planning of the party to me madam. You enjoy the party!" Before Sona could react, she had disappeared into the kitchen.

She then decided to really just sit back and enjoy the evening. She hardly budged from her chair, allowing Preeti to run back and forth with instructions to the kitchen. Rajeev mingled with the crowd, looking happy and content. Her fragile mother-in-law sat with some ladies, gossiping about life in the US and the different hobby classes she had joined. She was still slim and straight. "She had adjusted well to her life in the US and finally," Sona felt, "she was happy."

"Some people find happiness in the last few decades of their lives," Sona thought, "It is a kind of recompense for the sufferings they had endured in their youth." Geeta Jaykar had lost her youth to tragedy. Losing her husband as a twenty-six year old had been a blow that had almost finished her off. She was like an injured sparrow, trying to hold her own in a storm. But her father stood by her and her two sons grew up to be her devoted champions. If these men in her life had not been her supporters, she would have lost the will to live. She was incapable of fighting on her own steam, but her father, brother and sons rallied around her. Now she could look back at those unhappy decades of loss and emptiness without a pang. Life had taken away a lot when she was young, but in her autumn years, she was content and happy. Sona looked at her and unbidden the picture of her mother swam before her eyes. What storms had buffeted her when she was barely twenty-five! With what courage she had faced the difficulties! The men in her life failed her. Her father failed her by dying, her husband failed her by being who he was and her lover failed her by never checking back on her. But Mother was not an injured sparrow. She was a female eagle, soaring high, swooping and lunging through the strongest winds... Circling the valley to bring food for her young who depended on her. Sona's chin lifted up...Mother was a special woman. Sona had never organised a party like this for her mother. "I never gave Mother anything," Sona thought, with a pang, "Not even happiness."

The next morning Sona left for Mumbai.

27

Her state of mind on this journey to Mumbai was very different from her earlier journeys. She was looking forward to Mumbai... Looking forward to entering the Twenty First century. She did not look out of the window upon approaching Nasrapur. She could see it all in her mind's eye... The shuttered house, the haggard Station Master. She knew that Savitri was dead... A lingering illness that finally took her life. The Station Master had sent his two children to live with Savitri's parents. There they lived with their uncle and his wife and cousins and grandparents. He sent a definite amount of money to his in-laws' place and that took care of their schooling and clothes and other sundry expenses. They visited him on holidays and he visited them once in two months. They were intelligent children and though they had lost their mother, they were not orphans, living as they were in the heart of a busy household. The Station Master lived alone, with only the thoughts of his wife for company. He knew vaguely that he had failed her. "But how? In what way? Why was she never happy?" These questions lacerated him on lonely nights. Insomnia ravaged him and the house that Savitri had made into a home haunted him with her memories.

Sona did not want to see him. But she saw him nevertheless, hurrying as usual to the driver's cabin, dragging his legs, doing his duty, just doing his duty…

Sona went straight to the *Street* office from the station. Five days away from office and she was already anxious about how The Team had handled affairs in her absence. This was what she had christened her handpicked staff. They were a bunch of enthusiastic youngsters. What they lacked in experience they made up with their verve and energy. She had an open office, where they could pop in as and when. Unlike Fish-Eyes two floors below, she was very casual and friendly with her staff. Yet it was clear that she was the boss. They celebrated birthdays with cake cuttings and had regular outings to nearby picnic spots. The Team was her pseudo-family. Like a head matriarch, she ruled over her domain with an iron fist in a velvet glove. She knew their quirks and strengths. Almost all of them were coming to her raw. So she had to teach them, but the good thing was that they did not come with baggage, and she could mould them the way she wished. Not yet thirty and she sat in the Editor's chair. Mother would have been proud!What a relief it was to be in her cabin! She plunged into work, buzzing Govind for coffee and telling Sharon to bring in her article on college fests. She sent a message to Rajeev that she had reached safely and sent Preeti a thank-you mail. She thought of Preeti…her sweet, plump face, her chubby figure and the way she hovered around Rajeev, hanging on to his every word. Preeti even had Rajeev's saintly mother eating out of her hands. Literally actually! Her mother-in-law had reported that in the one week that it took Sona to reach Shivagaon, Preeti had prepared one special dish for her every single night. And every single night Rajeev had asked her to stay for dinner. At the party last night, her mother-in-law had automatically called for Preeti when she needed something. The house in Shivagaon was getting used to life without its mistress.

She turned back to her computer and was soon lost in checking in on pending mail. There was a mail from Nafisa. Her book on women politicians in India had been selected for a UN award, and she had been invited to receive it in Cairo. In typical Nafisa fashion, she had phrased the mail in understated words, but the magnitude of the prize which carried substantial award money was not lost on Sona. She immediately picked up her mobile and messaged Nafisa… "Congratulations pal! You should have called me up and given me this wonderful news! I am sooooo happy for you! Let's meet for dinner at The Loft… tomorrow…have a lot to share. Confirm ASAP!"

Nafisa came back immediately … "I have lots to tell you too. Some good, which you already know… and some bad…which I'll tell personally. Tomorrow then!"

Sona frowned. What had happened? Was Ammi alright? She had not spoken to Ammi in a long time. Sona looked at the time. It was almost one in the afternoon. Ammi must be in the kitchen. She punched Ammi's number. Ammi picked it up after only two rings. "Hello Sona! Kaisi ho beti?" For the next ten minutes, Sona allowed herself the luxury of listening to Ammi's gentle scolding and standard advice. Sona was relieved to find that Ammi was well. Slightly off-colour because of a fall she had had in the bathroom last week, but otherwise hale and hearty.

Sona kept down the mobile and called in Govind for further instructions on the meetings scheduled for the week. Govind was officially her PA, but so priceless that Sona often joked that his designation should have been 'trouble shooter'. He was a Mumbaikar through and through. He knew the heartbeat of the city. He had brought in news of incidents and happenings in the city almost before they took place, so tuned in he was to the rhythm of the metropolis. He had just graduated from a little known college. His English was so-so and the other staffers often ribbed him about his grammatical bloopers. But he was street-smart. For a magazine like *Street*, he was indispensable. Sona had slowly persuaded Mr Jeevan Prabhu to drop the elitist tilt of *Street* and had convinced him through the sales of the last two issues that making *Street* more inclusive, less Anglicized was the way forward. In this endeavour, Govind was her go-to guy. He provided the raw material. The other staffers polished it to a shine. The future was Govind. *Street* could not afford to by-pass his likes and dislikes. Mumbai was no longer Bombay.

Sona was fortunate in that she was a polyglot. She spoke three languages with equal flair-- English, Marathi and Hindi. These languages she not only spoke fluently but was an avid reader of literature in all three languages. She sometimes deliberately conducted morning meetings in Marathi. When Pesi Bandookwala, her Parsi Creative Head, protested, she just widened her eyes and said, "Pesi dear…your family has lived in Mumbai longer than mine has. Better pick up the local language!"

"But my Marathi is bai-wali Marathi!" sputtered Pesi, who had picked up whatever Marathi he knew from his household maid. They all laughed and Sona told him sweetly, (in Marathi!) that even bai-wali Marathi would do!

There was a call from Mr Jeevan Prabhu's office. The old patriarch wanted to meet Sona the next day. Sona fixed an appointment and wondered what he wanted to discuss. He was not the meddlesome kind, but he was totally involved with all the publications of *Swan*. In his seventy-fifth year, he was as sharp as when he started this publishing house. Sona respected his business acumen though sometimes she disagreed with him on his creative ideas. Sona had learnt that with Mr Jeevan Prabhu, it was best to be frank. He was a very secure and intelligent man. He did not discourage dissent. Infact he had that quality, rare amongst successful and wealthy men, of listening carefully. Perhaps that was the secret of his spectacular rise. He had started life as an ordinary bookseller, with a shop that he inherited from his father. Without any fancy degrees from foreign universities, he had started Swan Publishing. With every new publication, his stock rose. And now, he had scores of MBAs working for him. Oxford educated scribes and Harvard educated marketing professionals. Swan was now a media house and Swan House was a multi-storied building in the commercial heart of Mumbai. It was prime property and Sona had been given a posh office on the top floor.

Sona got up and stood by the window. The grey sea could be seen in the distance, the waves heaving noiselessly as she watched from the confines of her air-conditioned office. She felt happy and successful. "Wish Mother could see me now," Sona thought for the hundredth time.

28

The next evening, Sona was already at The Loft at eight. Govind had reserved the best table for them. He knew the maître d'hôtel. Sona sat near the window, overlooking the glittering city below. She ordered one of the interesting mocktails that The Loft was famous for, and she picked up a green olive from the bowl the waiter placed before her and popped it into her mouth. She eased back into her chair and allowed the strains of the music to waft around her. Feeling relaxed and content, she sank back in her chair and awaited the arrival of Nafisa, who was uncharacteristically late. Sona took a sip and looked around at the genteel ambience of the restaurant. The maître d'hôtel hovered around her. She was known at the restaurant. The Manager came up and made small talk. Waiters were discreetly deferential. Sona checked her mobile to see if there was any message from Nafisa. What was taking her so long? Then, she saw her... saw Nafisa coming towards her like an angel. She was wearing a flowing long white kameez of some chiffon-like material and her white chiffon dupatta fluttered behind her like an angel's wings. She came towards her with a slight smile on her pale angular face. Her family traced its lineage back to the royal family of Junagadh and all that refinement, that nazakat could be seen in her gait, her face, in the way her jet black hair bounced healthily as she walked.

Treading lightly, she came towards the table where Sona sat and Sona got up and embraced her friend warmly. "After such a long time Nafisa!" she sighed. "It has been ages since we met and exchanged notes. Now just sit back and tell me all that's happening in your life."

Nafisa sat down and ordered her drink. She took a sip and looked at Sona.

"Khaled is going away," Nafisa said.

Sona looked at Nafisa quickly. For the first time, Sona noticed that her eyes were haggard and lines of pain were etched on her face.

Sona took her hand in hers. "But you were expecting this, weren't you?" she asked. "This would have happened one day. Khaled would eventually leave. That was an understanding between you two, wasn't it?"

"That still doesn't lessen the pain," Nafisa said, bending her head.

Sona looked at her friend with compassion. "Off-beat life choices demand a strong heart Nafisa," she said, "When is Khaled leaving?"

"Much before we had expected or hoped. He had applied for a post at the University in Dubai. He had given an interview through video conferencing a week back. Today, he got their mail saying that he had been selected. He has to join by the beginning of next month. That leaves only a fortnight for us."

Nafisa looked at her, her eyes heavy with tears. "Nafisa, control yourself. You have got too emotionally involved in this relationship. He is *not* your husband you know."

"He is more than that," Nafisa said, a tear rolling down her cheek, "He is my first love. He is the man who validated my existence as a desirable woman. He is the man who made me feel cherished and loved. And now he is going away."

"There is something called a long-distance relationship you know," Sona said.

"Not with Khaled," Nafisa said, "It will either have to be that we marry and live together or that we go for a clean break. He said as much."

"Well then, a clean break it will have to be!" Sona said, suddenly annoyed, "Nafisa, it was very, very foolish of you to get so emotionally involved in a relationship that already came with an expiry date."

"I couldn't have given my body without giving my heart!" Nafisa said, looking at her plaintively. Sona's heart was wrung to see what love could do to a confident and balanced woman like Nafisa. "She will get over it," she thought with compassion, "Each day the pain of not having Khaled with her will lessen and one day will come when she will not think about him the whole day."

"Let it flow then," she told Nafisa, "Cry my dear, and get it out of your system."

Nafisa wiped her beautiful eyes and said, "No crying now. Let us celebrate my award! Cheers Sona! My dear, dear friend!"

They both took sips of the excellent mocktail and smiled at each other. Driving back to '1, Sagar Apartments', Sona thought about Nafisa and Khaled. The two were so well suited for each other. Nafisa had blossomed in the last two years since she met Khaled. She looked youthful, lovely and happy. For that at least Sona was grateful to Khaled. But then, her heart hardened at his ultimatum and the difficult choice he had given Nafisa. Nafisa deserved a kinder man.

Back home, she changed and on an impulse dialled the landline of Shivagaon. Rajeev must be back from the factory. She had not spoken to him yet. She had just sent him a message. It was not right to take your husband so much for granted. He was not Khaled. She wanted to tell Rajeev, "Rajeev, whatever the reasons for our living apart, I am proud to be your wife and I miss you." She had not said such loving words to him for a long time. It was true that he had not said such words to her either. But this was not some kind of an ego competition. She dialled the landline number of her Shivagaon home. The phone rang and rang and Sona was about to keep the receiver down when it was picked up. "Hello," said Preeti's voice. "Hello! Hello!" Preeti repeated at least three times before Sona could react.

"This is Sona. Are you having dinner?"

"Hello Sona Madam," Preeti said, "We've finished dinner. Jaykar Madam has gone up to her room. Rajeev Sir and I were having coffee in the porch outside. That is why it took some time for me to pick up the phone. Any problem madam?"

"No problem Preeti. There does not have to be a problem for me to call up my husband at this hour. Please give the phone to Rajeev."

There was silence then and sounds of shuffling and whispering and Rajeev came on the line.

"Hello Sona, any problem?" He repeated.

Sona lost her cool then. "Do I have to call you only when there is a problem? Can't I call you for no reason at all? Does everything in life have to have a reason?"

Rajeev was silent. Then he took a deep breath and asked quietly, "Why did you call?"

"It doesn't matter now," Sona said, "Goodnight."

She kept down the phone and tears sprang to her eyes. Her gaze fell on the photograph kept on the side table... A profile of her mother. It was taken by Henry Bassinger, the famous photographer from *Life*. They had done a cover article on Mother. Sona loved this photo. It epitomized Mother... Beautiful, strong and alone. Mother rarely smiled in her photos. There had been no one to give Mother the gift of a smile. Solitariness had been her hallmark. Perhaps that is why she had so passionately wanted Sona to stand on her own feet and have a career before plunging into marriage. Ultimately, there only yourself you could depend on. Happiness and unhappiness were within you. You had to feed your own core and make it strong. Only then could you offer anything to the world. Mother was a giver. That is why her constituency elected her again and again. Mother gave all to the world around her. And the world, looking at the strong and confident woman, forgot to ask if she needed anything in return.

29

Sona was packing to leave for Delhi. The Ministry of Youth Affairs had organised a three-day Symposium on 'Challenges before the Youth of India' and a whole lot of academicians, media persons, young achievers and activists had been invited to present papers and have panel discussions. As Editor of a youth magazine and as a young achiever herself, Sona had been invited to be a part of a panel discussion too. Though the delegates had been booked into a decent three-star hotel, which was close to the venue, Sona had booked herself into Taj Palace on SP Marg. She had set herself a date to start work on Mother's biography. It was time to interview Brigadier Vikrant Singh and she wanted to do it without the prying eyes of the other delegates hovering over them.

She booked herself a cab from the airport and drove to the Taj. It was late at night. She had taken the night flight from Mumbai. As soon as she came into her room, she just changed and settled into bed. She was tired. It had been a full working day and it would be a full working day tomorrow as well. She looked at her watch. It was 10:30 at night. The next day, she had to be at the venue by 9 am. She set the alarm and closed her eyes. Just then, her mobile pinged. It was a message from Brigadier Vikrant Singh. "Have you reached?"

"Safe and sound", she typed back, "in bed. Eyes wide shut!"

"Good girl! Will meet you tomorrow. Will let you know the time. Good night."

"Good night VS!"

She closed her eyes and was instantly asleep. A blanket of peace and protection covered her.

The venue next day was teeming with delegates and security personnel. The Union Minister for Youth Affairs was coming for the Inauguration. All the delegates were seated on time. Sona sat with a group of media persons from Delhi. The Inaugural Function was a typical Delhi affair, reeking of formality and protocol. The day's schedule stretched till five. There were to be two sessions after lunch break, punctuated by a coffee break. As the delegates streamed out of the hall for coffee after the first post-lunch session, Sona saw a familiar figure far away. He stood out because of his height and his erect posture. Sona's heart skipped a beat. They saw each other at the same instant and moved towards each other simultaneously. Then Sona looked around self-consciously and checked her stride. Almost at a leisurely pace, she strolled towards Brigadier Vikrant Singh and gave him an excited smile. He took her by the elbow and whispered, "Let's leave!"

"But there's one more session to go," she said.

"Let's leave!" he repeated and escorted her firmly towards the entrance.

They walked briskly to the car park and it was only after they were driving through the spacious roads of Delhi that she turned to him and asked, "Where are you spiriting me away in such a hurry VS?"

"I'm taking you to a place that serves the best coffee in the world. And the bonus is that you won't have to pay for it by sitting through another boring panel discussion."

She giggled girlishly. "Will I be able to interview you there?"

He looked at her, and punched her playfully on the shoulder, "You can interview me as much as you want, madam journalist!" he said, smiling fondly.

They were seated at a discreet corner of the café. It was a trendy joint in Hauz Khas. The crowd around was arty type and casual. "You look really out-of-place here, V S!" Sona joked.

"Yaar, don't always push us faujis into terrorist-infested jungles. You civilians can't be the only ones enjoying the prosperity of India, while we faujis sweat it out on the borders! In any case my dear, I don't look as out-of-place here as these over-fed guys will look in the forward areas."

"Oh chill V S! I was just teasing!"

"And you do it so well!"

The coffee and sandwiches arrived and she took a sip of the excellent brew. "Why are you so silent V S? You want to tell me something? Is that why you brought me away in such a hurry?"

"Swaroop is leaving for Canada at the end of this academic year." His voice was flat. Sona looked up at him quickly. His face was impassive.

"Oh V S!" she said, "How could she do this to you?"

"She is an autonomous being. She is free to choose where she lives and with whom."

"But V S! Your kids! You love them! They will move away from you!"

"They are almost adults now. Ready to fly the nest in any case! They will soon make their own decisions. As for me, I will ask for a posting to a field area again. I don't need a family station, when there will be no family!"

Sona looked at him hurriedly and was upset to see that he was trying hard to keep his emotions in check. She clasped his hard hand in her soft palms and looked at him with love and compassion.

"You are all the family I will have then Sona," he said.

Sona got up swiftly and sat next to him. "Oh V S! V S!" She said, as she kissed his hand, "You will always have me! Always!"

"Sona," he said holding on to her hand tightly, "I can't tell you what a source of strength you are to me! What a pillar of support! I need you Sona! Need you! Promise that you'll never leave me!"

"I'll never leave you VS, come what may! We will always be there for each other!"

It was only after he was driving her back to her hotel that she turned to him and said, "Hey VS! What about my interview? When will we get time to do that?"

"I will come a bit early from office tomorrow and pick you up during your lunch break. We will have lunch somewhere and then you can interview me. You decide the venue."

"The lobby of the Taj! A discreet table, away from prying eyes."

"Ok my dear! Your wish is my command!"

"I hope my bunking of sessions does not get me into trouble with the organisers!"

"No fear! You can charm your way out of any situation, can't you?"

She giggled. "My panel discussion is on the third day. Morning session. Interested?"

"I will try." He smiled at her. He himself was the author of a well-appreciated Report titled, "Induction of Women in the Indian Army: Challenges and Changes." Gender sensitisation in the Armed Forces was a topic close to his heart. Through interaction and discussion with Sona, he had learnt a lot about the gap between the changing aspirations of India's young women and the aged policy makers, who sought to slot them in traditional roles. As the Editor of a successful youth magazine, Sona was in a position to give him the latest update on India's youth. Inspite of the difference between their ages, Sona was always amazed to see how respectful he was towards her opinions. He was never condescending. He broke all the stereotypes she had harboured in her mind about Army types. He ribbed her sometimes, but did not treat her like an air-headed youngster. He had said many times that if he was a decorated soldier, she was an award-winning journalist too. He was a very emancipated man and in spite of being in a male-dominated profession, acknowledged that India could never move forward without including women in all areas of development. Policies would have to change to make the workplace more inclusive. Sona talked to him passionately about this and he listened with an attentive air. Exchanges between them were never boring. He was a well-read man and often found himself without a sparring partner amidst his Army colleagues in the intellectual debates he ran in his mind. And now, he had found Sona. With Sona, it was different. She was bright. She was witty. She was sensitive. And…he had to acknowledge this…she was pretty as a picture!

They walked into the lobby of the Taj. Sona took his arm proprietarily. He caught a sight of them in the full-length mirror at the entrance. They looked so well together.

He looked down at her and happiness welled up inside him. "You are beautiful!" he whispered and she blushed deeply.

"Don't leave immediately!" she said to him, her eyes big and fluttering, "Let's sit in the lobby and have a drink."

They sat and ordered lime and soda and spent another hour in each other's company. Both were reluctant to say goodnight. Brigadier Vikrant Singh seemed strangely vulnerable today. And Sona felt strangely protective about him. It was as though their default roles were reversed. He was leaning on her and she was giving him support. They sipped the lime and soda and talked to each other in low tones... Almost intimate. Then he looked at his watch and got up. "I must leave. You take care Sona. I'll come for you tomorrow."

Just as she said good night to him, she stopped him again and said, "But VS! What about my interview?" They looked at each other and smiled.

30

The next day, he was waiting as promised. She edged towards him as unobtrusively as she could. They sauntered off casually towards the parking lot and as soon as they reached it, ran towards the car like excited teenagers. He started the car and sped out of the venue. "Where are you spiriting me away today Brigadier Vikrant Singh?" she enquired laughingly and laughingly he replied, "To a place that serves the best Punjabi food in the world!"

They drove to the outskirts of Delhi and then on the highway he stopped at a place. "Come!" he said, "The tastiest kaali daal and sarson ka saag you can imagine!"

She saw that it was a roadside dhaba. There were charpoys set outside. Most of the customers were truck drivers and villagers. She could not spot a woman anywhere. But she was not afraid. She was with a paratrooper. The guy could kill with a single blow. She felt safe and secure with him, safe enough to venture into the darkest gullies of Delhi. The owner of the dhaba saw Brigadier Vikrant Singh and came out. "Jai Hind Saab!" the old Sardar said.

He was an ex-serviceman and knew Brigadier Vikrant Singh.

"Madam is coming here for the first time," Brigadier Vikrant Singh said, indicating Sona, "Make her happy!"

The old Sardar smiled and hollered to his boys.

They sat on charpoys and ate the wonderful rustic fare, which was served in thalis, and washed it down with tall glasses of buttermilk.

"That was wonderful VS! Better than any five-star's fare! The weather is lovely isn't it? And the country air so pure! I almost wish we did not have to go back to the pollution of the city!"

"There's no hurry to go back, is there?" he asked.

"Not really."

"Then let's just enjoy the ride!"

They drove in silence for a kilometre or so and then he pointed to a large spreading tree close to the road. "Nice interview spot?" he asked and she smiled and nodded.

He parked by the side of the road and took out a dhurrie, some cushions and an old shawl. He spread the dhurrie on the shady grass patch under the tree and sat down, leaning against the tree trunk. She sat on the cushions. "Okay…" he said, settling comfortably, "Get into your journalist mode now."

"Where did you meet Mother and what was she like? Tell me about your school, your railway colony, your neighbours… I want to recreate it all in my mind… the atmosphere of that place. I am not recording what you are saying VS. I will remember all that you say."

He started speaking then. She sat before him, nodded, smiled, and laughed at the witty way he sometimes described things. She lay down on the dhurrie and looked up at the blue sky and allowed his deep voice to wash over her. The main road could not be seen from where they sat. Far away, she could see a few huts and some human forms, small as ants. The sun filtered in over them in dappled spots and illuminated his face in horizontal lines. His short cut hair clung to his shapely skull and his handsome face looked animated as he spoke. She kept looking at him and the way the sun danced off his tanned features. He was looking into the distance and speaking, delving into his past and recalling moments, which he himself had almost forgotten.

"What a pair of monkeys we were Sona," he laughed, but got no response. He looked at her. She was fast asleep. She was lying on her side, facing him, with her face resting on her palm. A stray tendril of hair whispered over her forehead. She looked like an angel, the bloom of youth on her face. In her pink tee and blue jeans, she lay sweetly dreaming, oblivious to the world. He smiled to himself, dusted the old shawl and spread it over her. Tenderly he brushed away the stray curl from her forehead and sat back again, waiting for her to awaken.

31

It was eight in the evening. The Team had already left the office premises. The building security guard had peeped in once, wished her and left. Sona had taken to spending two extra hours after office, working on Mother's biography. She wanted to release it on her second death anniversary. She already had a contract. It was a major publication house. They were excited about it and were pushing her every day. They wanted pictures and that was a big job. Pesi was helping her with the old photos she had managed to salvage from Mother's albums and old stacks of photos, and she was also recruiting the help of sundry cousins and forgotten relatives in sourcing childhood pictures of Mother. The book and its subject consumed her now-a-days. In death, Mother was closer to her than she ever had been in life. Sona worked like a possessed being. Sleep, hunger, aches and pains were forgotten as she laboured on. She had not called or met up with friends and relatives for weeks and weeks. Only those who bothered to call her got a response. Pesi had digitized some photos that she had selected and she was checking them on the computer when her mobile pinged. "VS!" the screen flashed.

"Go home now Sona…It is late!"

"How did you know I'm in office?" she typed.

"I called up your home…Shevanti told me. This is not okay. You should go home on time, eat on time, sleep on time…" the letters came slowly.

"Yes Sir!"

"Seriously, Sona! I get worried for you…there is no need for you to drive yourself like this!"

"It is the fag end of the book. The deadline is close. I want it to be a wonderful book. Don't you want it to be a wonderful book VS?"

"I want the book to be wonderful", he typed back, "But more than the book, I want my wonderful Sona to remain wonderful… which she will not if she neglects her health like this."

"You are sweet VS", she typed, "Sweet of you to worry. Nobody has worried for me like this ever."

"So shut your computer and get yourself back to '1, Sagar Apartments'. Shevanti has made puran-poli today, you know that?"

"Didn't know!"

"Off you go, girl!"

"Okay boss! Who can refuse Brigadier Vikrant Singh? Bye."

"Take care…call to say goodnight."

"I will."

She shut her computer and came out. The Security at the gate saluted her as she drove out. She was tired and hungry. If VS had not goaded her, she would probably have stayed for another hour. But he was right, she was probably over-doing it.

Back home, she got an earful from Shevanti as well. Shevanti prepared wonderful puran-polis. It was her signature dish. And she wanted Sona to give it the respect it deserved. Sona ate hungrily and then locked up after Shevanti had cleaned the kitchen. She dragged herself to bed and typed a message to VS.

"Goodnight girl!" He typed back immediately, "Sleep well and sweet dreams!"

"Good night VS!" she typed, "You sleep too!"

She then turned on her side and closed her eyes. Sleep came like a loving parent, enveloping her in its warm folds.

32

Sona had just finished her morning meeting when she got a call from Mr. Venugopal. He was working as the PA of another Minister in the same Party now. But each time he called her, he cried about Mother. Mother's death had been a blow to him. Personally, because she had handled him with care and consideration and professionally, because she had been a rising star. Her death meant a professional setback for him. He now worked for a minor Minister and his personal equation with him, from what he told Sona, was not the same as it had been with his dear Madam. Now on this sunny December morning he called her excitedly to tell her that Mr Upadhyaye, the Party chief, wanted to speak to her about a Very Important Matter. He made it sound like a state secret that should be guarded with one's life. She heard him out and promised to get back to him. Then she awaited the call from Mr Upadhyaye. The senior politician was a shrewd old man. He had been Mother's mentor. Her untimely death had devastated him. He was planning big things for his protégé. After her death, her constituency could not be regained by the Party. Her constituency had voted for the person, not the Party.

Soon enough Mr Upadhyaye was on the line. He had a proposal for Sona. He wanted to induct her into the Party. Elections were a year away. As Mother's daughter, she could nurse her constituency. The Party would nominate her from there. Sona was stunned.

"Upadhyayeji", she protested, "I am not my mother. I am not cut out for politics. I am a simple girl and I want to lead a simple life. I respect you, but please don't ask me to join politics."

"Only you can take your mother's place Sona," Mr. Upadhyaye said, "With the passing away of your mother, we have lost an invaluable Party functionary. We want to reclaim her constituency. If you stand for elections, I am dead sure you will be elected. The Indian public is still feudal in thinking. Their loyalty towards your mother would be transferred to you. Imagine Sona, you will be one of the youngest MPs in the Lok Sabha. Does anyone get a head start like this?"

"Mr Upadhaye, I am *not* interested in politics. I want to lead a quiet life. Away from the public glare. My mother was an exceptional woman. I am not her!"

Mr. Upadhyaye was quiet. He was not used to being refused. "Promise that you will think about it then," he said. She promised that she would.

But after she kept down the phone, she was shaking. A storm rose in her heart. She was her mother's daughter. But she was *not* her mother! When would the world realise this and leave her to be Sona Jayakar? She could not concentrate on her work that day. Her old insecurities came back. Her past haunted her and she felt again as she had felt whenever she followed Mother to her functions sometimes... A pale imitation of Mother... Trying to live up to impossible expectations.

Sona wanted to discuss this with someone. Someone who knew her inside out... Someone who knew her insecurities and her complicated relationship with her mother. She picked up her mobile.

"Hello Nafisa?" she asked.

Nafisa was at her desk, going through a student's PhD chapter. She looked at the mobile a bit crossly. But when she saw 'Sona' flashing on the screen, she picked it up immediately.

"Hello Sona! Where have you been my dear? How do you remember me today?"

"Oh come on Nafisa! I always remember you! It is just that I am overwhelmed lately with work on Mother's biography. The deadline is closing in and I don't want to be late."

"You won't be Sona. But you sound disturbed. What's the matter?" Nafisa was being astute as ever.

"The Indian Democratic Party wants me to contest the next elections from Mother's constituency."

"Sona!" Nafisa almost shrieked with joy, "That's wonderful! What a fantastic opportunity!"

"Wonderful? Fantastic?" Sona was taken aback with Nafisa's reaction, "This is me we are discussing here! The most unlikely person to be a politician! Do you even know me? I have been under immense pressure since Upadhyayeji called me up. He does not like to be refused. What would you have done if you'd been in my place?"

"I would have grabbed the opportunity with both my hands," Nafisa said promptly. "Sona, you nitwit, somebody as shrewd as Upadhyayeji will never make an offer before thinking it over carefully. He obviously thinks that you have it in you to wrest that constituency back into the fold. He can't think of any other woman who would be able to win it back."

Sona kept down the phone thoughtfully. Thoughtfully she punched Upadhyayeji's personal mobile number. He picked it up almost immediately.

"Haan beti!" he said, "Kya socha hai?"

"Upadhyayeji, I am too small to fill my mother's shoes. Also, I am not cut out to be a politician. Infact, because of the circumstances of my childhood, I have an allergy to politics."

"So…you refuse me!"

"Nahi Upadhyayeji. I have thought of somebody better than me for that seat. More qualified, more able, more efficient and more dynamic."

"Hmm…who is it?"

"Prof Nafisa Ahmed!"

There was silence for a while. "I've heard the name," he said, "Read it in the papers. She is a senior academician... Professor of Politics at Mumbai University. She was in the news recently. Her book on women politicians has won some kind of award hasn't it?"

"You are right!" Sona said, enthusiastically, "She is perfect for the job Upadhyayeji! I will campaign for Nafisa! She is willing to join politics, I know that."

"Okay… Speak to her and then get back to me. If she is showing interest, I will call her tonight."

Sona kept down the phone, her eyes shining. That went well! She picked up the phone and called Nafisa again. Nafisa was just about to finish reading the chapter that her PhD student had written, when the ring of the mobile intruded into her thoughts. "What the hell!" she muttered and picked up the phone.

Sona again! "Hello Sona! Again! You don't call me for weeks on end and then you hound me with calls after every twenty minutes! You are a strange one!"

"Nafisa, you won't believe what I have to tell you!"

Sona launched into a detailed account of the conversation she had had with Upadhyayeji. "And so…" she ended breathlessly, "What do you say to it?"

"I think I say yes!" Nafisa said, and laughed out loudly in her excitement.

"Let's meet at my place for dinner this weekend. Shevanti will cook up something special."

"Ok buddy!" said Nafisa, "You are my soul-mate, d'you know that?"

"I am just your friend," Sona laughed, "I don't believe in these fancy things like soul-mate and all!"

"Well friend! Let us meet at your place at 7 this Saturday! Got a lot to report! On other fronts too!" and Nafisa signed off.

Nafisa had been toying with the idea of joining politics for a while now. She was convinced that educated and sincere people were needed to bring about a change in society. Indian politics had slipped into the hands of the greedy and the opportunists. They had made a joke of democratic elections... Religious politics, Caste politics, class politics, language politics, regional politics, river politics. Anything that could be milked to garner votes were fodder for the unscrupulous politician. And the educated class just looked away...suffused with cynicism. But she wanted to be part of a mainstream political Party. She knew she would be nowhere as an Independent candidate. In spite of her idealistic views, she had a realistic take on modern day politics. The thought of using Sona as a means of introduction to her mother's Party had never occurred to her. But when Sona herself broached the subject, the offer was too good to refuse.

Sona kept down the phone and sent a message to Upadhyayeji about it. Then on an impulse, she picked up the phone and called up Shubhendu.

He picked it up almost immediately. "Sona?" he asked, his voice incredulous.

They had not been in touch for a long time. In spite of working in the same building and the same organisation, Sona seemed to be systematically avoiding him. For what reason, he was unable to fathom. But now with her call, he was completely taken aback.

"After so long…" he said.

She agreed ruefully. "I am calling you to invite you to my place for dinner Shubhendu. This Saturday, 7 o'clock."

Shubhendu agreed, though he was still perplexed when he kept down the phone. He had never visited Sona at '1, Sagar Apartments'. Their friendship belonged to the poverty-stricken stage of Sona's, when she lived in a rented flat, when she was alone and friendless, and when she was a junior working under him. '1, Sagar Apartments' belonged to the new stage of her life. The posh apartment in an up-scale locality belonged to a Sona he did not know. She hob-nobbed now with senior politicians and Army officers. She called home the likes of Mr Jeevan Prabhu. He, Shubhendu, was a small fry in her bright circle of friends. The days were long past when she came over to his house on Sundays, with her hair freshly washed and clutching a plastic bag filled with fresh vegetables. Forgotten were the endless games of Scrabble they played and the back-to-back movies they saw on his prized giant size TV. Forgotten too were the mock-punches he threw at her when she goaded and teased him mercilessly and the popcorn she threw at him when he became too sentimental with some movie scene. This Sona was different... An entirely different being. She had changed after she came back from Delhi after her mother's funeral. She was catapulted into another sphere. She moved into a new neighbourhood. She moved into a posh office. She moved into the Editor's chair. She moved away from him. She was no longer the simple Sona he knew. But out of the blue today, she called him. And he agreed. Because it was difficult to refuse this Sona. She was imperious, just like her mother.

Sona smiled happily when she kept down the phone after speaking to Shubhendu. He did not know Nafisa well. She, Sona, was the only common link between them. It was time to introduce them properly to each other. If Nafisa wanted to win the elections, she had to start courting the media. And it would start with Shubhendu. If Shubhendu took a shine to someone, he would go that extra mile to write a wonderful article. He wrote beautifully, eloquently. His pen had the power to influence opinion and turn the tide. Nafisa could do with some help from Shubhendu!

She left office earlier than usual on Saturday. The cooking was being handled by Shevanti. Raghu had dusted the drawing room as instructed. Sona stopped to buy fresh flowers at the neighbourhood florist. Long expensive stems of tiger lilies, yellow roses and a lot of ivy creepers. She arranged the flowers tastefully around the room and twined the creepers on the backs of chairs and across the mantelpiece, their dark leaves gleaming devilishly in the subdued lighting. She thought nostalgically of her home in Shivagaon where she performed this ritual of arranging flowers with almost religious fervour. She thought of her garden that yielded different flowers in different seasons. She missed the feel of the earth in Mumbai. She missed the gardening, the landscaping project that she had started and that was abandoned halfway when she came away to Mumbai. Now the garden survived, but it did not flourish. She could sense its benign neglect and the way Ganpat had allowed it to go to seed. Yet, the last time she had been in Shivagaon, when her mother-in-law was around, there were other issues weighing on Sona's mind and the garden and Ganpat's laziness were pushed to the corner of her mind. But now the picture of her carefully nurtured garden falling apart rose before her eyes and she could not suppress a sigh of regret. "That Ganpat needs a dressing down", she thought to herself, "Rajeev is too preoccupied to check Ganpat's laziness. Champabi is the only one who is actually earning her keep. What work does that lazy Ganpat do?"

She arranged the tiger lilies on the mantelpiece, distributed the dozen yellow roses in two vases, and placed them in the corners of the room. She lighted tea lights in their hanging holders and went to her room to freshen up and receive her guests. She was putting the bottle of sparkling wine in the ice bucket when the doorbell rang. It was Shubhendu with a box of Bengali mithai. She welcomed him warmly and just as they were exchanging pleasantries, Nafisa came with a bottle of red wine, packed in golden paper and tied with a pink satin ribbon. They hugged and she walked her friend in. Nafisa was a bit taken aback when she saw Shubhendu in the room. She had expected to be alone with Sona. They shook hands and asked formally about each other's welfare. Long ago, Nafisa had warned Sona about "That middle-aged Bengali babu, who is out to seduce poor innocent Sona!" And Shubhendu always referred to Nafisa as "the pseudo Mother Teresa Nafisa Aunty!" Both were actually meeting each other face-to-face for the first time. "Ironical that the guy who had given that memorable name, 'Idyllic Female Paradise' should take so long to meet her best friend," thought Sona. Both were witty conversationalists. But now, they just sat there looking at each other, stupidly replying in monosyllables and giving false smiles. A strong dose of sparkling wine was urgently needed! Sona left them in the drawing room and went into the kitchen to get cashew nuts and olives. She fetched the wine glasses and expertly popped open the cork. When she took the tray into the drawing room, the two were in the midst of an animated debate. Shubhendu shaking his head violently and Nafisa gesturing with her hands. Sona smiled to herself. The wine was not even needed! The evening would be a success!

Shevanti had prepared prawn biryani, daal fry, dahi vada and zeera alu. She brought hot rotis to the table when they sat down to eat. Her semolina kheer was excellent. Shubhendu, who had a sweet tooth, and a nice little paunch to prove it, had multiple helpings of the warm, dry-fruit encrusted kheer. Later they sat out in the balcony, sipping coffee, hearing but not seeing the heaving dark Arabian Sea in the vicinity. The cool December breeze tickled them languorously as they sipped the wonderful coffee Sona had brewed. "The best meal I've had in ages," Shubhendu declared, and Sona warmed to him and wondered why she had avoided meeting such an openhearted man. Nafisa was in high spirits too and Sona was glad that she was gradually forgetting Khaled and his possessive ways.

Shubhendu left soon after coffee and Nafisa lingered a while. "What did you want to tell me Nafisa?" Sona asked, and Nafisa looked at her and shook her head in disbelief.

"You know Sona, this was the first evening after Khaled left that I have not cried for him."

Sona patted her hand. "Soon he will only be a memory Nafisa! A very pleasant memory perhaps, but a memory nevertheless. You have to move on in life na, my dear! You can't survive on memories alone!"

"Yes", Nafisa said, swallowing a sob, "We have to move on… Khaled will take a long time to vacate my heart! The stubborn bastard!"

33

The much-anticipated day dawned. The book was to be launched at the hands of Mr Upadhyaye. Clarion Publishers had pulled out all stops to make the arrangements perfect. Mr Venugopal was already at the venue, supervising the preparations. Rajeev was driving over from Shivagaon. Brigadier Vikrant Singh had already arrived. The final copy, which was to be released today, lay on Sona's desk. It had been produced beautifully... Hard-back. On the cover, she had used Henry Bassinger's portrait of Mother. It was in black and white. The pictures inside were spanning her entire life, right from grainy, sepia-tinted pictures of her babyhood to the by-now-famous very last photo. It showed Sona lighting the funeral pyre of Mother as hundreds of people stood around to say their final goodbye. This photo, by Abhinav Shukla, the photographer famed to have captured pictures of all important political events in India in the past forty years, had been splashed on the front page of all newspapers. Sona fingered the book lovingly. It was a thick book and writing it had been physically and emotionally draining for Sona.

The subject of the book was a woman whose many hidden facets were unearthed only as Sona dug deeper and deeper into her past. Sona had prepared a short but emotional speech for the event.

Everything seemed to be in order. She called up Mr Venugopal to make enquires and he was quite enthusiastic about it. He was taking a keen interest in the launch. This was a book on his dear Madam. Whatever he was today was because of her encouragement and support. This tribute to Madam had to be done gracefully, befitting Madam.

Sona arrived at the venue an hour before the arrival of the Chief Guest. She was dressed in a creamy-white sari and was wearing delicate gold ornaments. The creamy-white colour on chiffon material offset her dark complexion beautifully. The officials from Clarion Publishing briefed her about the sequence and Mr Venugopal briefed her about the other arrangements. As the time for the launch came nearer, her heart fluttered and there was a squeamish feeling in the pit of her stomach. As she sat there reviewing the sequence, she felt somebody sitting down next to her. "Hi!" said Brigadier Vikrant Singh. He looked dapper indeed in his white shirt and dark trousers. Sona widened her eyes in glee and clutched his hand in excitement. His face broke into a grin. "All set, my girl?"

"All set sir!"

Then things became a bit of a blur as people started arriving and she had to get up and move about meeting all and sundry. She was again surprised and overwhelmed at the number of lives Mother had touched and goodwill she had built. All these people were here because of their love for Mother. They had no other selfish motive. If Mother had lived, she would have gone far in her political career. When Mr Upadhyaye arrived, activity reached a fever pitch and security personnel sprang into action. The dais was beautifully decorated. The function got off to a good start. A few bouquets were handed over, Mr Upadhyaye spoke a little, Mr Kewal Pratap of Clarion Publishing spoke a bit and then Sona spoke a bit. Then the book was formally released. It was an emotional moment for Sona. It was a day when the book was launched. It was also a day when Mother had breathed her last breath, two years ago. As she sat on the dais, Sona's eyes roved over the audience. Seated amongst the milling crowd were the people she was looking for... Nafisa in the second row, sitting with Shubhendu... Rajeev in the front row, talking to a Minister sitting on his left. Sona looked around. Brigadier Vikrant Singh sat in the front row too, a few chairs away from Rajeev. All her people! Hers! They were here for her! Tears welled in her eyes but she checked them. "Mother, Mother," she thought, "you should have been here!"

The function was over. The book was flying off the sales counter set up near the exit. The Team was efficiently supervising the sales. Pesi had mounted a beautiful display on a board behind the sales counter. The Team was doing this for her. It was not part of their job to help in the sales of the book. But ever since Sona declared her intention of writing the book, they were backing her, helping her, going out of their way to speed up the project. Today, on the day of the launch, they were looking as proud as she was. Sona saw them from afar. Pride and thankfulness rose in her heart. The publisher had given her a few complimentary copies. After Mr Upadhyaye left, the formality and tension in the hall eased a bit. She came down the stage and mingled amongst the audience. Mr Venugopal brought forward her complimentary copies and Sona went straight to where Brigadier Vikrant Singh sat, solitary and erect. She sat next to him and picked up the first copy from the stack of books in Mr Venugopal's hand, touched it to her forehead and handed it over to him. "Thank you!" Brigadier Vikrant Singh said, and flipped open the book. It opened on the first page. In fancy typeset, it said:

"For Brigadier Vikrant Singh... VS... my dear friend and collaborator, without whose help, this book wouldn't be *this* book!"

34

It was Mother's fourth death anniversary. Sona had got used to a world without Mother. The Team had left for the day. She was alone in office. There was no incentive to go home. There was no one waiting for her, not even Shevanti who had gone to her in-laws' village for her first delivery. There was a temporary cook in her place for the time being. She came in the evening, cooked dinner and left. Sona would come home, microwave the bowls and take her dinner plate in front of the TV. It was a solitary affair. However, she did not think this with sadness, but with resigned acceptance. This was a life she had built. And if someone had asked how she was faring, she would have said, "Fine!"

And fine indeed it was! Ever since she had won the Wordsmith award for her book on Mother, in the 'Best Non-Fiction Category', she had been toying with multiple possibilities in her mind about what to do with the substantial prize money. Now she had thought of something. She wanted to bounce the ideas off someone. She picked up her mobile.

"Hello, Nafisa?" She said.

Nafisa's 'hello' sounded preoccupied when she picked up her mobile, but as soon as she heard Sona's voice, she perked up. "Sona!" she exclaimed, "What's up dear?"

"Hi Nafisa! Are you still in office?"

"Yes Sona, clearing files."

"It is late. Aren't you hungry?"

"Aren't you? But the cook must have prepared something yummy for you."

"Yeah, and Shubhendu must have prepared something yummy for *you*!" Sona said.

"Yes! Fish curry and rice. He is determined to convert me to macher jhol!"

"Well, you've married a Bengali! You better start loving your fish!"

"Oh", Nafisa said, affectionately, "I love the fish and the fish-maker!"

"You are lucky Nafisa" Sona said, fervently, "You have an emancipated husband, who thinks nothing of taking the back seat and being your support structure. Nafisa, cherish him! Such men are rare!"

"I know Sona," Nafisa said, "I send thanks to God every day for giving me Shubhendu! I was made for him and he was for me! And look how long it took us to find each other!"

"But at least you found each other!" Sona said, unable to keep the wistfulness out of her voice, "Sometimes, years go by, and you never unite with your Other!"

There was silence on the line for a while. "How is Rajeev?" Nafisa asked after some time.

Leena Chandorkar | 223

"He is fine. Travelling a lot," Sona said, "Look Nafisa, I wanted to talk to you about something. Can we meet somewhere over dinner?"

"Sure," Nafisa said, "The Loft it is!"

"Wonderful!" Sona said, enthusiastically, "Tomorrow, 8 PM, you and me, dinner date at The Loft!"

It was the usual table for the two of them at The Loft. The table near the window, overlooking the glittering city below. Govind was very particular about making advance reservations. As usual, Sona was the first to arrive. As usual, she ordered a new mocktail. And as usual, she sipped a glass of it while she waited for Nafisa. Nafisa arrived straight from office, wearing a cream Bengal cotton sari. How elegant she looked in spite of putting in a full day at work! People turned to look at her as she walked in. As Minister of State for Education, her face appeared frequently in newspapers. Sona's promise to Mr Upadhyaye about the appropriateness of Nafisa for Mother's vacated seat was justified by the immense hard work Nafisa was putting into her job. She knew her limitations of course, but her in-depth knowledge about the workings of educational institutions gave her an insider's insight that previous ministers had lacked. Her commitment to her constituency was clear by her frequent visits to the place and her accessibility. Her charming personality made her immensely popular with the youth and the womenfolk. It was the men, the older men, whom she found hard to win over. But by giving to them the deference which they were traditionally used to and which they took for granted as their due, she was able to charm them as well. Sona had campaigned tirelessly for her during the elections, appealing for votes using the emotional factor to the hilt. Nafisa had to win! This was Sona's obsession, and she was happier than Nafisa herself when Nafisa romped home with a thumping majority.

As Nafisa settled into a chair and sipped her drink, she raised a quizzical eyebrow at Sona. "What was it that you wanted to speak to me about, Sona?" she asked.

Then, Sona told her about her dream of starting the Kamala Pradhan Polytechnic for Women in Mother's constituency, (for that is how she thought of the constituency though Mother was no more!) As Minister of State for Education, Nafisa was in a position to expedite the project and help her immeasurably in other ways. Sona told in detail about the form of the Polytechnic, the immense value it would have for the rural young women, and the need for quality educational institutions in rural areas. Nafisa listened patiently and declared herself totally impressed with the proposal.

"Draw up a project outline Sona," she said, "I will see to it that this dream project of yours sees the light of day very soon."

Driving back to '1, Sagar Apartments' that night, Sona felt like patting herself on the back. How right had been her advice to Mr Upadhyaye! How suitable was Nafisa for the job! Nobody else would have been able to fill that empty space left by Mother.

Nafisa worked day and night to prove herself fit for the job. She had a number of things to prove to a number of people. But most of all she did not want to disappoint Sona's faith in her. Nafisa thrived on the job. She, who had lost her spark after Khaled's departure, recovered it again after she started first to campaign for the seat, and then later, to prove herself worthy of it. In the interim, her association with Shubhendu increased, deepened. It changed its colour. They moved from being mere acquaintances to being friends to being lovers and then to being mates. Being married to Shubhendu anchored Nafisa emotionally and physically. His solid support gave her immense energy to move forward and ambitiously she worked hard, burnt the midnight oil and strove to be the best that she could be.

Sona came back to the apartment and quickly changed into her nightwear. It was late and she was tired. She checked her mobile for messages. There were none. VS was posted in a forward area. Network connection was often unreliable. They sent each other e-mails and tried to keep contact. But it was not so easy. Sona thought of him often, with a lingering pang. It seemed to her that he was punishing himself for something. His family was in Canada now. He was effectively alone. That emotional day in Delhi when he had clutched Sona's hand and told her never to leave him, seemed to have been an aberration. Now, even when Sona sent him half a dozen mails, he would reply with one brief, succinct mail. It generally mentioned that he was fine and he hoped that she was fine as well. It rarely went beyond pleasantries. Those three days in Delhi when he had seemed so vulnerable, needy and emotional were like a dream... forgotten. Sona did not know what to make of him. He seemed a tortured soul, but was refusing her hand of friendship. She wanted to help him but he was intent on keeping his distance. Finally, exhausted, Sona had scaled down her communication to him too. Now she wrote to him only when she felt the energy to do so.

She lay her head on the pillow, exhausted but strangely wakeful. She turned to look at the picture of Krishna she had placed on her bedside table. He was her favourite god from the Hindu pantheon and epitomized for her all that was open, liberal, and inclusive in her religion. Though she was not ritualistically religious, she found nowadays that her belief in her faith gave her a courage that she sorely needed. It was a beautiful picture, which Nafisa had sent her. Sona had framed it and kept it next to Mother's photograph... the one that Henry Bassinger had taken. Now she picked it up and looked at it long and longingly. Krishna looked back at her, smiling and benign. "All will be well Sona!" he said, "Sleep!" And Sona lay her head on Krishna's lap and slept.

35

Sona was working on the project outline for the Kamala Pradhan Polytechnic. She was unable to concentrate. She felt strangely restless today. She felt that she was on a treadmill, going fast nowhere. With a shock, she realised that ever since Mother's assassination, she had not taken a holiday at all. She was drowning herself in work, trying to submerge into her subconscious, half-finished issues that needed closure. But instead of addressing them, she was picking up ever new projects to immerse herself in.

Finally, unable to bear the oppressiveness in her mind any more, she picked up her bag around four o'clock and told Govind that she was leaving. She could no longer bear being in the close confines of her office. She drove herself to Galaxy Mall. It was the biggest Mall in India. It was posh, huge and sinfully luxurious.

She was very disturbed. She just wanted to lose herself in the crowd and blow up an obscene amount of money on something totally unnecessary. Mother would not approve! But Mother was dead!

Sona headed towards Nazakat Creations. Their designer saris were to die for. She would splurge on a sari that she totally did not need!

She entered the posh interiors of the exclusive designer store where saris started from Rupees thirty thousand apiece. Owning a Nazakat sari was the dream of every bride. Though Sona was not a bride, she wished to indulge herself today. She entered and a smart young salesman greeted her immediately. "May I help you Madam?" he asked with false obsequiousness.

He made her sit down and asked her what she wanted to buy. As she told him what came first thing into her head and he scuttled off to find the required saris, she looked around the exclusive showroom. There was only one more customer in the shop, a woman, who was sitting on the other end of the store. She looked in that direction and her heart started beating fast.

Looking intently at bridal lehengas was Preeti! She was deep in discussion with the smart saleswoman who was catering to her.

"Preeti?" Sona mouthed to herself. Then, clearing her clogged throat said loudly, "Preeti?"

Preeti turned and looked towards her. The colour on her face came and went and Sona saw that she went white, as though she had seen a ghost. Sona walked up to her and said, "Preeti?"

"Madam? What a surprise!"

"What are you doing Preeti?" Sona asked.

"Shopping for my trousseau…" Preeti said, turning red.

"Oh, Preeti!" Sona said, "How wonderful! Who is the lucky guy?"

Preeti looked down. "It is an arranged match madam," she said, "My mother wanted to see me married before the year end. She is not keeping well. She has been after me. She keeps saying that she will not die in peace if I do not marry soon. She had given me an ultimatum. This man is from our community. He is based in Kuwait. He is a widower, and father of two kids."

She looked up at her, her eyes dull with pain.

Sona reached out for her hand. "You are not happy Preeti?"

"A poor girl has no choice."

"You are not poor Preeti. You have a good job. You are taking care of yourself and your mother."

"I have no autonomy," and a tear rolled down Preeti's cheek.

"Preeti!" Sona exclaimed, "Come, let's go and grab some juice or coffee in the café downstairs."

Sona threw a charming smile at the salesman, who had just come up from the basement with a handful of saris and with a "We'll soon be back!" she and Preeti walked out of the exclusive confines of the designer store.

Sipping a café latte each, Sona looked at Preeti. She hardly looked like a blooming prospective bride. If anything, she looked like a ceremonial lamb being led to slaughter.

"Do you have his photo?" Sona asked.

Preeti fished into her bag, brought out her mobile and showed her the picture of her fiancé. Sona saw a decent looking Gujrati guy, smiling amiably at the camera. He looked neither too young, nor too old. In fact, he looked just right for Preeti, who could hardly be described as a kacchi kali herself.

"He is good-looking," she said.

Preeti said nothing.

"Why are you not happy with the alliance Preeti?"

Preeti looked down and a sob came from her.

"You love someone else?" Sona asked.

Preeti looked at her with terrified eyes.

"And does that someone love you too?" Sona asked softly.

"He is not available, not free to be mine," Preeti said, swallowing with difficulty. "He is a man of honour. For him, duty comes first. He is the kind who will sacrifice his love for duty." She looked down and repeated, "He is not free."

"And suppose he becomes free?" Sona asked, her voice a whisper.

Preeti looked at her with pleading eyes.

Sona reached out and took her hand in hers. "Preeti," she said softly, "I will talk to Rajeev tonight. There is no need for you to thrust yourself into a loveless marriage."

Sona got up swiftly and almost ran out of the café. She got into the lift and reached the parking lot. Inside the car, she started the engine and just sat like a stupefied doll. Then jerking herself awake she drove out of the silent parking lot.

Back home, she threw herself on her bed. Lying face down and burying her face in her pillow, she bawled till her tears had made it damp. After crying like this for some time, she sat up, feeling much the better. She looked at the time. Rajeev would not be home yet. There was no point in calling him up with this dangerous call while he was at work. She decided to wait for him to be home, and to be back in his room after he had had his dinner.

She got up listlessly and changed. The new maid popped in to ask what she wanted for dinner. But she said that she would skip dinner tonight. She simply had no appetite left. Around nine, she called up Rajeev. But the network was acting up and she was not able to get through. After several false tries, she sent him a message. She worded it carefully. "Rajeev", she typed, "If your heart is elsewhere, I set you free to be with someone you truly love. I am not the kind of possessive wife who will cling on to her husband and show ownership rights when it is obvious that he wants to be with someone else. Rajeev, a marriage contract cannot be a noose around one's neck. We do not own each other. We are autonomous beings and I will respect your choice if you decide to move away. Just say the word and I will let you go!"

She pressed the 'Send' button and a tear rolled down her cheek. She blankly kept watching the TV programme she had put on and then finally put it off. She walked into her bedroom and lay down. She looked at Krishna again, "Give me strength," she said. Taking the picture to her heart, she closed her eyes.

36

It was around two in the night when she was disturbed by the ringing of her mobile. Groggily she looked at it. "Rajeev", it flashed. Her heart missed a beat. "Hello", she croaked.

"Open the door!" Rajeev said, "I'm outside!"

She got up swiftly and ran to the front door. Looking out of the eyehole, she saw him standing outside. She unhooked the safety chain and unlatched the door. Rajeev came in, roughly pushing her aside.

He walked straight to the drawing room. He looked dishevelled, tired and extremely agitated. He pulled out his mobile and thrust it in front of her.

"What is the meaning of this?" he asked.

'Rajeev,' she read, 'If your heart is elsewhere…' Blankly she re-read the message she had typed five hours ago. It sounded brutal and heartless. She looked at Rajeev, whose eyes were heavy with unshed tears.

"I met Preeti today," she stammered, "she said, she said…" and Sona sat down and hiding her face in her hands started crying.

Rajeev let her cry for some time.

"Preeti said something and you wrote me this devastating message! Sona, is this the trust you place in me?"

He came and knelt down beside her. "Sona", he said softly, "Don't make this an excuse to get out of this marriage. Is *your* heart elsewhere? Are you tired of me?"

"No Rajeev, no!"

"Then why did you write this? Do you think that you know everything? That just because I let you be, I do not care for you or for your welfare? You cannot take all the decisions regarding our relationship. I am not a demonstrative guy, Sona. But have I ever, through word or deed, let you feel that my heart lies elsewhere?"

"But Preeti said…"

"Forget about what Preeti said!" Rajeev said, suddenly angry, "This is about us! Did *I* say anything? I cannot control Preeti's feelings. I can only speak for myself. Sona, my heart is with you… In your safekeeping. You do what you want to do with it."

He laid his head in Sona's lap. Sona put her arms around him and felt his warm tears soak her lap. Her tears dropped over him and they stayed like this for long. He got up after some time and turning her back to her went and stood by the window, staring out into the darkness. Sona went up to him and clung to his back. "Hold me then, Rajeev!" she said, "Never let me go!"

It was impossible for them to go to sleep after this emotional scene. She was frightened to see Rajeev so upset. She had never seen him shed a tear in his life. It lacerated her heart to see that she was the one responsible for his tears now.

"Will you have cheese toast?" she asked him. He smiled ruefully at her and said yes.

She went into the kitchen. He did not follow her. He was not brought up to be very handy in the kitchen. Men's and women's spaces were well-defined in the world he was raised in. And the kitchen was a woman's domain. She put the coffee in the filter machine and brought out the cheese slices and bread. Her mind was blank, but she prepared this midnight feast with great love and care. She cut the perfectly browned cheese toast into triangles and put them on a white, dainty plate. She arranged the plate and coffee mugs neatly on a tray. She put paper napkins on the side and carried the tray to the drawing room. Rajeev was standing by the window again, looking out. She placed the tray on the centre table and he turned at the sound, then came and sat on the sofa. She picked up a triangle of toast and extended it towards him. He took a bite of it and then she took a bite of it too. He placed a hand on her cheek and said, "Put this mad idea forever out of your mind Sona. There is only one woman for me, and that is you! All the Preetis in the world cannot take me away from you."

They fed each other the triangles of toast until all the triangles finished. He sipped the coffee and said, "Only you can make coffee just the way I like it Sona."

She laughed and said, "Oh, your dialogue-baazi! So unlike you Mr Rajeev 'Serious' Jaykar!"

They sat next to each other, close and snug and talked softly till day broke across the sea. He had driven his black Mercedes as fast as he dared all the way from Shivagaon to Mumbai, the moment he got her message. It had been the darkest, saddest journey of his life. What had made Sona feel so forsaken and alone? Why had he not been there for her? After her mother's assassination, she had drifted away from him. Why had he allowed his ego to surmount his love? In his flight to success, in his mad pursuit of ticking off all the boxes within the given time, he had forgotten that life was a river... A river with unexpected bends and turns. To be prepared for the unexpected was half the battle won. Why had he forgotten to hold Sona's hand in his flight to success? And why did he not extend his own when she needed it most? Wracked by unanswered questions, he drove fast, his black Mercedes cutting through the silent darkness. He was angry... Angry more with himself than with Sona. He was half-afraid that he had already lost her... Lost her to somebody else. Somebody she found more sympathetic. So, when she opened the door in her white nightdress, he could not stop himself from shaking her, shaking her hard till her curls fell across her small, dark face.

37

It was the inauguration of the Kamala Pradhan Polytechnic for Women and Sona was a bundle of nerves. She was the Director of the Polytechnic but the day-to-day working of the Institution would be handled by a Principal she had appointed--an efficient lady who had served earlier in administrative positions in Management Institutes. Dr Sarla Wankhede was selected not only for her formidable leadership qualities but also because of her commitment towards the upliftment of rural women. Nafisa and she hit it off instantly. Nafisa saw in her a kindred spirit. Nafisa told Sona in private that if there were more committed women like Sarla Wankhede, India would be a different country indeed.

The inauguration of the Institute was to be at the hands of the Chief Minister of Maharashtra. Nafisa, as the sitting MP and a close friend of Sona's, was the Chief Mentor of the Institute. Nafisa had laughed when Sona proposed this designation for her. "Even without giving me this fancy designation, I would be a support to this Polytechnic Sona," she had said, "I am totally for the idea as you have put it. And now, after meeting Dr Sarla Wankhede, I see that dream of yours coming to realisation very soon!"

Sona's plan of vocational training for women in the Polytechnic sprang from her desire to fulfil

Mother's dream of empowering women, especially economically backward and rural women. Women had always worked. But this training would give the power directly into their hands, giving them confidence to stake a claim on 'their' money. They would be trained to start small businesses and carry out simple banking procedures. The girls in the village rarely left the village for further studies unlike boys. The village high school made them literate but did not equip them for jobs. In fact, there were no jobs for them in the village. The Polytechnic would train them to create their own jobs, have their own businesses.

Sona had got a call from VS on the morning of the inauguration. He was now posted somewhere in the Eastern sector. He was doing very well in his career, but repeated in his mails that if God had blessed him professionally, He had been rather stingy as far as his personal life was concerned. Sona reassured him many times that there were plenty of people to love him. Often, she was the one offering emotional support rather than the other way round. But he seemed less tortured now and was reconciled somewhat to the changes in his personal life. Swaroop and he had separated legally a couple of years ago. She was working in a hotel now in Canada and from what he gathered from his children, she was happy and glowing as never before. His children were in college in Canada. They kept in touch with him and had visited him last summer. The adjustment to the changed family equation had been most difficult for him, because it was he who had been left alone. Yet, now he felt closer to Kamala than he had ever felt in his entire life. This new venture of Sona's had impressed him no end and he had sent her a long, loving mail commending her considerable energy and verve. He poured out all his own energies into his job, bringing to it an edge of selflessness that was rare. Sona told him often that she wanted to see him in the highest post and he always laughed and said that that was hardly the motivation that drove him. Yet, it was true that he was climbing the slippery ladder of promotions in the Army quite steadily and that too without treading on too many toes.

Thus, VS was not present physically but his mental support gave her courage. The nitty-gritty of the Inaugural Function was being handled by Rajeev. He was busy supervising arrangements for the event. His PA was running around like a headless chicken. He was new to the job and out to impress his boss with his dynamism. Preeti had resigned and was now happily married and settled in Kuwait. On a short visit to Shivagaon, Sona had extracted this information from her ex-colleagues. She had not attended Preeti's wedding but had sent her an expensive wedding gift... A beautiful designer sari 'With Best Compliments from Mrs Sona and Mr Rajeev Jaykar'! She sincerely hoped that Preeti was well adjusted in her new life and when she heard that Preeti was doing well, she was genuinely happy.

The substantial Wordsmith prize money did not seem so substantial once the work on the Polytechnic started. There was a considerable government grant that would help in the initial stage, but it was Sona's desire to see the Polytechnic become self-sufficient as soon as possible. There was space enough for a dairy farm of its own, its own poultry farm, its own jam and pickle making factory and a small manufacturing unit for making clothes. This would be a training ground for the girls as well as a means of generating income for the Polytechnic. Sona had already met the villagers when she had campaigned for Nafisa. Now, she had had a meeting with the Sarpanch and other important village bigwigs and convinced them about the importance of training their girls. When the benefits of educating their girls were laid out to them in clear economic terms, it became easier to win them over. She spoke to the girls who had finished their tenth standard. They were bright girls with the spark of youthful energy in their eyes. Most of the SSC toppers were girls, but it was ironical that the only fate for them was to wait for the right moment to get married. When she spoke to them in private, their dreams, their yearnings, their longings came across to her. They too wanted to stake their claim to the economic success of their country. They too wanted a role beyond the traditional role of wifehood and motherhood. Their desire for an autonomous existence was what touched Sona deeply. She spoke to them passionately from the bottom of her heart, about the importance of being autonomous beings. Of how this would not be contrary to being good wives or mothers. Of how, in fact, it would empower them to be better daughters and wives and mothers as they would be helping in the economic improvement of their families and most importantly, equipping themselves with a say in matters. What fascinated the girls the most was the fact that Sona had driven all the way from Mumbai all alone in her own car.

"How did you come to our village madam?" they asked.

Sona pointed to her SUV parked outside.

"Who drove?"

"I drove."

"There was no man accompanying you?"

"No."

The girls looked at her with renewed respect. She doubted if they would have taken her seriously if she had come chauffeur-driven in a luxury sedan. She looked so totally in control of her mobility, her life, that it was impossible not take her as a sterling role model.

The Inaugural function had to be a grand affair. Sona was a politician's daughter. She understood the importance of symbolic gestures. She had invited all her media friends to the function. Her friends from the Press and from TV were special invitees and they were covering the function with all the respect it was due. The CM, by gracing the function, had already lent it a stature that was undisputed and now Sona hoped that the additional publicity would give the Polytechnic the required push to make it a sought-after destination for rural girls from all over Maharashtra. She had built a hostel that was safe, affordable and clean. It was within the pristine confines of the campus and the fees charged were negligible. Infact, she had provided accommodation in the campus hostel for all out-station students. This was one of the major reasons why parents were willing to send their girls to the Polytechnic. Sona's own personality and the reassuringly strict personality of Dr Sarla Wankhede played a vital role in persuading the parents that their girls were in safe hands.

The final result of all this ground work was that by the time the day of the inauguration dawned, all the seats for the first batch of students were filled. Sona's faith in the success of the Polytechnic was validated by the presence of the village people, all the guardians of the students who had taken admission and the girls themselves sitting demurely on one side of the audience in their uniform of navy blue kameez and white salwar and dupatta.

"My pioneering batch!" Sona thought, pride swelling her heart, as she looked at the sixty girls from the dais. The CM gave a thundering speech on women's empowerment and everybody clapped till their palms hurt. Nafisa, in her capacity as the sitting MP, gave a short but sincere speech. Then, it was Sona's turn. She started mundanely enough, but as she came to the elucidation of the name given to the Polytechnic---Kamala Pradhan Polytechnic for Girls----her voice suddenly broke and she veered away from her prepared speech and gave a passionate speech on Kamala Pradhan and why this Polytechnic would be the best gift to her memory. The CM, who had been a close associate of Kamala Pradhan's, was seen wiping his tears from his eyes and the TV cameras dutifully captured this touching scene. Sona herself could hardly keep the tears from her eyes and what she spoke was so sincere, so heartfelt, that there were very few dry eyes in the audience after her touching speech was over.

Rajeev drove back the same night for Shivagaon and all other guests from Mumbai zoomed off too. Nafisa left as well. Sona had decided to spend the night on the campus. There was a guesthouse on the campus, where she stayed that night. After dinner, she strolled towards the girls' hostel and spent an enjoyable two hours in their company. Young girls who were barely 18…19…but so full of optimism, hope, verve. She came back to the guesthouse feeling energised and elated. All would be well! Mother and her indomitable spirit would see that this Polytechnic with her name given to it would not only survive, but flourish!

38

Sona was all in a tizzy. She could not concentrate on work in office. She kept calling up Shevanti to see if things were going according to order. Finally, irritated, Shevanti told her to leave office and come home!

"Sorry Shevanti! Won't disturb you again!" Sona said, subdued, and got back to her computer.

VS was coming to Mumbai! He had retired as a Lt. Gen. after a glorious service in the military. His last posting was as the GOC-in-C of Eastern Command. It was an emotional day for him when his men gave him a ceremonial farewell. His excellent equation with the Chief Ministers of the area irrespective of their Party affiliations had allowed him to implement his anti-militancy plans without any hiccups. Militancy had come down drastically during his tenure and it was attributed to his carrot and stick approach. He was firm, yet he also gave a patient ear to the problems of the militants. The media just adored him. Though Sona herself had never carried out an article on him, many of her friends in the media had. VS was always careful to attribute his success to his team. Never did he try to hog the limelight himself. That endeared him to his troops and kept envy out.

And now, he was coming! She was meeting him after a long gap. He was planning to stay in Mumbai for a week and then he had to go back to Delhi to finalise details about his new assignment. Sona had taken two days' leave from office on the last two days of his stay. He was arriving tonight from Kolkata and as usual, Sona was going to pick him up from the airport and bring him home for dinner. He was putting up in the Army Mess during his stay but tonight he had promised to give quality time to Sona.

Sona had a long conversation with him on the day of his retirement. He was not hanging up his boots in a hurry. The government had appointed him as India's Ambassador to Israel. Before taking on the new job, he wanted to come to Mumbai to spend some time with Sona and to finalise the possession of his new apartment. It was in a Housing Society quite close to Sona's and it was at her insistence that he had done the booking two years ago. It was a new Housing Society. "I'm a man of the hills Sona, I love it in the hills" he had said when Sona had excitedly told him about the bookings being open.

"What are you going to do all alone in the hills, my dear VS?" Sona had exclaimed, "You need your family around you, don't you? And I'm all the family that you have in India, my dear General!"

"The Army is my family!" retorted VS, ever loyal.

"Oh yes, it is! But it doesn't have a face! And it doesn't make you laugh the way I do!"

"Nobody can win against you in an argument!" he exclaimed.

Two days later, VS had transferred funds and Sona had paid the initial booking amount. Sona bullied him a little and he gladly allowed her to bully him, dropping his strict fauji demeanour and laughing freely at all her jokes. He had sold his ancestral property in the hills to a hotel chain, which paid him a neat amount for the scenic location that the erstwhile home of the family was situated in. It was the location that fetched the handsome price. VS gave it up with a pang. But he had decided to be practical and pragmatic. Neither of his two children was ever likely to come back to India. Why hold on to a property where no one would ever live? And Sona was right. The spot was too isolated. He did not want to be cut off from society in his advanced age. Sona was a comfort, his only family, the one he felt closest to now. She was more than family. Family consists of people we are tied to through bonds of blood and social contract. Sona was somebody he had felt connected to immediately. It was a bond without a name. She had aroused in him all the deep feelings that he had thought he had buried when Kamla died. And so he allowed Sona to rule over him. She wanted him near her... And near her he would be. In any case, he would be in Israel for the next three years. After that, who knew what Destiny had in store for him!

Sona called out to The Team that she was leaving for the day. She wanted to freshen up and then go the airport at 7 o'clock.

He was one of the first to come out from amongst the passengers in his flight. He always travelled light, with only cabin baggage. He stood out from a distance. Except for the fact that his face was gaunter and there was more salt than pepper in his hair, he had not changed much from the VS she had met during Mother's last days. Her heart brimmed with joy upon sighting him. He waved to her and they almost ran towards each other. She gave him a hug in her usual warm way. Sona was a reserved person, but with people she loved, she was very demonstrative, never stingy with hugs and embraces. VS came late into her life, but their connection had been immediate and deep.

Once at '1, Sagar Apartments', he relaxed. Shevanti had surpassed herself with the dishes. She liked VS. He treated her with unusual courtesy and relished all her dishes. She insisted that he should have another hot roti and he ate heartily.

Later, as he and Sona sat in the breezy balcony, eating the dessert of rice kheer, she enquired about his children. "They are fine, fine!" he said. Then almost casually, he said, "Did I tell you? Swaroop has remarried?"

Sona looked at him quickly, with disbelief in her eyes. But his face was impassive. "Well, she says that he is her soulmate. Most importantly, according to her, he does not come with past emotional baggage. That's a jibe at me, by the way!"

He looked up at Sona and gave a lop-sided smile. "I'm glad she is settled. Michael is her boss at the hotel where she works. He is a divorcee with two kids as well. Hope that she is happier with him than she was with me."

Sona reached out and took his hand in hers. "It is Destiny VS! You are a very lovable guy. Only, Swaroop and you were not meant for each other."

"I know". He shrugged, "I did not hold on to the one who was meant for me!"

They were both silent then, looking out into the inky darkness, with the distant roar of the sea lending poignancy to the moment.

She had taken leave for two days only for VS. She helped him choose an interior decorator who promised to do up the interiors according to the brief given by VS. But even in this he was guided by Sona. "You have excellent taste Sona. You decide," was what he would say whenever the interior decorator asked whether this was better or that. Finally, it was decided that work on the interiors would start in a week's time and whenever the decorator had any doubts he was to ask Sona rather than disturb General Saab!

Lt. General Vikrant Singh stood in the sea-facing balcony of his house looking out into the distance, his eyes dreamy. Sona came and stood next to him. She nudged him playfully. "Wake up General! Welcome to your new house! Not as grand as the appointment bungalows you are used to perhaps, but adequate enough for one old man, eh?"

"Who is old?" he growled, playfully biting her bare shoulder, and she giggled.

"Come out of your reverie then," she said, snapping her fingers, "Tell me, what colour walls do you want in this room?"

He allowed himself to be led by her, walking from room to room, looking more at her animated, lively face than at the blank walls she was pointing to...

39

Sona was in Shivagaon. But according to her daily habit she got up automatically at 5:30 am. She reached out to feel Rajeev, but he was already gone. He got up at 5 am everyday and went for his regular long jog. Then came and worked out with his weights, prepared tea and read the newspapers thoroughly... Three newspapers--- a business newspaper, a National newspaper and one local newspaper to keep him abreast of events closer home. Then he had fruits---three varieties of fruits, which Champabai had been instructed to always keep stocked. Then he took a bath, did a short puja and had breakfast. At precisely 7:45, his driver drove his black Mercedes out of the gates of the house. He arrived at office at 8... always 8! You could set the clock by the arrival of Rajeev Jaykar into the premises of *Geeta Engineering Works.* Even when Sona came to Shivagaon during her increasingly rare and short visits, he did not vary his routine. It was only when his mother had visited Shivagaon that he had slackened a bit and varied his tightly programmed day. When Sona complained about this obsessive discipline with a pout to her mother- in- law, Geeta Jayakar had laughed charmingly and said that this strict punctuality was something that was in his DNA thanks to his father, the legendary Maj Raghav Jayakar.

Now, when Sona got up automatically at 5:30, she looked around, disoriented. Instead of the pink walls of her bedroom in '1, Sagar Apartments', she saw the ivory white walls of the house in Shivagaon. The large painting of the New York City skyscrapers that she had bought when she visited that wonderful city hung on the wall opposite.

"You're on holiday, Sona," she chided herself, "You can loll in bed for some more time." But it was more tedious to stay in bed thinking all kinds of thoughts than to be up and about. So she hauled herself out of bed, slipped her feet into her slippers and went and stood by the upper-floor bedroom window from where she could see the garden below.

It was Ganpat's garden now... To be neglected or cared for as he thought fit. Gardening was not one of Rajeev's passions. He hardly bothered about what grew in it and what did not. Sona's eyes were attracted to the little mound in the corner of the garden, covered with green grass and wild flowers. What caught her attention were the numerous yellow butterflies that were flitting over this mound. This was the abandoned rock garden. The rock garden that Sona had planned years ago. Soon after that, Sona had shifted to Mumbai. And then she had been sucked into her other life. The aborted rock garden remained…a dug up corner of the garden, piled high with a tempo-full of soil that she had ordered. But after that, work on it had stalled. The pile of soil stayed there, sprouting grass and wild flowers as seasons changed and months passed. Rajeev left it to

Ganpat to do what he wanted with it. Ganpat, being chronically lazy, had done nothing. Sona, whose baby it actually was, had abandoned it halfway. So, there it stood, a blot on the otherwise beautiful face of the garden. "Projects should not be abandoned half-way," Sona thought, "There should be a closure."

This was the first time that this thought had occurred to her. During her earlier visits, all through the intervening years, the abandoned rock garden had hardly caused her any uneasiness. It was happily thriving in its corner…home for many insects and sundry garden animals. A wild patch in the otherwise carefully landscaped garden.

Around 11 in the morning, when she took her mug of coffee to the garden and stood in front of the wild patch, thinking over what to do with it, a car turned into the driveway. It was Pushpa… Making an impromptu visit as only she was allowed to. They hugged and after Shevanti had got her a mug of coffee too, the two friends stood in front of the half-finished rock garden again.

"I want to finish this project Pushpa," Sona said, "It was years ago that I conceived it. Nobody bothered with it. It just lay there, half-dug, waiting for further improvement."

"Well, it looks fine to me!" Pushpa said.

Sona looked at her quizzically.

"It is the very wildness of the patch that is interesting Sona. Nature has worked its magic on it. See how lovely it looks! A little hillock in the corner of the garden, covered with green weeds, wild flowers, little burrows made by little garden creatures. Notice how all the butterflies are hovering over this mound. You have allowed a part of your garden to thrive as Mother Nature wished it to thrive. Leave it! It is a refreshing contrast to the rest of the finished garden. Not everything need be controlled Sona. You should let go too. Allow nature to take its course. It adds charm to the landscape!"

Sona recalled her visit to Japan a few years ago when she was at *News*. She had gone to a Japanese garden. It was autumn. The trees were flaming orange and red. The shrubs were precisely clipped. There was a whole section of bonsai trees. It was unbelievably clean. What stayed with her was a scene that she witnessed. There were gardeners moving around with scoops. The moment a leaf fluttered down on the perfectly manicured lawns, they would swoop down and collect the leaf. The landscape was pristine again! The garden, though exquisitely beautiful, had left her cold!

Sona looked at Pushpa. Pushpa sometimes said such profound things! That was why she was her favourite person in Shivagaon.

Now as the two friends stood side by side and looked at the little mound overhung with flitting butterflies, Sona started looking at it from Pushpa's perspective. Really, come to think of it, it was not a scar! It was infact Sona's offering to Mother Nature. It was true that it had a wild air about it, but it also had a gay charm... A careless abandon about its beauty.

"This is what I am!" it seemed to say, "Love me if you will, or gently pass me by!" There did not seem to be an urge in the patch to be loved at any cost. It just was! Ganpat was very happy with this patch. It never asked to be weeded or watered or sprayed with insecticide. It just thrived and changed colour according to the seasons. How in tune it was with the seasons!

"You are right Pushpa," Sona said, "We should let nature take its course sometimes. We should not always try to control the flow of the river. Let it flow… take its course, through bends and turns. I will leave this patch as it is. A testimony to the wild beauty of nature!"

40

Sona had taken a week off from work to be at Shivagaon. For a change, she had taken this leave not for somebody or something, but only for herself. She just wanted to relax, unwind. Things at *Street* had stabilised now. The Team was quite capable of handling things without rushing to Sona for every detail. Over the years, *Street* had created a niche for itself in the market, clawed its way to the top and the list of its advertisers was impressive enough to bring from Mr Jeevan Prabhu praises for Sona. True to his promise, Mr Jeevan Prabhu had never interfered in the daily affairs of the magazine. He had given his young editor a free hand and had only been in the background, offering support and help when needed. Sona had fulfilled the vision he had had from a magazine for the youth, and because of it she had become a regular in the lavish parties he threw in his sea-facing mansion. There he invited famous writers, journalists, publishers and media persons from all over the world. Though Sona was the kind who did not much fancy partying, she could not refuse Mr Jeevan Prabhu's invitations. There she came in contact with all kinds of celebrity authors and media people. It was fascinating to listen to them and hear their tales of exploits amidst war zones, political intrigues, red carpet events and important conferences.

Actually, though *Street* was Sona's project, it was now safely on its feet, showing healthy financial returns, and frankly, it had lost its challenge for Sona. She was unconsciously looking for another challenge, another project. She wanted to move on to some other place.

Perhaps this brief holiday would give her some direction. She had talked about her feeling of restlessness to Rajeev and he had suggested a week away from all the hustle and bustle to a quiet retreat in the mountains or by the sea. She, who had not taken a holiday for years, felt it to be an almost impossible indulgence but the more she thought of it, the more it appealed to her. "Why not?" She thought. It had been a long time since Rajeev and she had taken an exclusive holiday together. They were both settled in their careers now. They both deserved the break.

But why had she not taken a break? What was driving her? She was trying to prove something to someone. To whom? As long as Mother was alive, Sona had always been in conflict with her. Nothing that she did pleased Mother, and so she had given up trying and slowly had started rebelling. But with Mother gone, Sona had become her own harshest critic. She had to excel in everything. And she was doing well in almost everything that she started. Unlike her poor father, all that she touched was turning to gold. But there was no Mother to applaud her.

Rajeev was in office when he got a call from Sona. "When are you coming home Rajeev?" She asked.

It was a simple question. But his heart leapt with joy. It was 7 o'clock. Most of his office staff had gone home. They had families waiting for them... Wives, husbands, children, aged parents. But he worked late. He usually worked late. There was nobody waiting for him at home. Dara had got used to his long timings. So when Sona asked him when he would be home, he said, "Right away darling!"

When his black Mercedes turned inside the gate, he saw that the garden lights were on and so were the lights inside the house. As he got out of the car, he saw Sona come out into the porch. She was in her pink kaftan, which was a shapeless garment that he had never liked. But today, seeing her figure silhouetted under the porch light, he thought that he had never seen her look so charming. Dara as usual, bounded up to him with a short, hearty bark and Sona waited for him to reach her. He pressed her arm and only said, "Sona!"

They both turned inside the house which had come alive with the flower decorations that Sona had put in their usual place.

He changed into comfortable clothes and came down. Sona was waiting with the tea tray in the porch. He felt blessed. He took the cup of tea she poured out for him and reached out for a piece of dhokla that Champabai had prepared. They sat quietly in amicable silence sipping tea and enjoying the view of the garden. Dara sat next to Rajeev. Rajeev looked at Sona's face and felt a surge of emotions. "Stay here in

Shivagaon Sona! With me! Please!" He was surprised at the pleading note that his voice had taken.

In response, Sona only took his hand in hers and pressed it gently.

"Tell me," she smiled, "where would you like to go for a holiday? Amsterdam?"

They watched the twilight fading from the sky and the darkness slowly enveloping the garden... and then like magic, one by one, the solar lights that Rajeev had installed on the garden bushes came to life...lighting up one corner of the garden and then the other...dispelling the darkness...*tamso ma jyotirgamaya*...

----------------######----------------

About the Author

Leena Chandorkar grew up as a cantonment child and studied in different schools across India. She did her graduation in English Honours from Lady Shri Ram College, Delhi and acquired her PhD in English Literature from Pune University. She is the author of the book, *'Eye Me Myself: A Study of Six Women's Autobiographies'*. She teaches English at Garware College, Pune. *Bends and Turns* is her first novel.

www.ingramcontent.com/pod-product-compliance
Lightning Source LLC
Chambersburg PA
CBHW020727210626
46807CB00016B/364